Escaping the Tiger

Escaping the Tiger

Laura Manivong

HARPER

An Imprint of HarperCollinsPublishers

The author gratefully acknowledges Maya Angelou for permission to reprint the quote on page vii, from *Words of Hope and Courage*.

Escaping the Tiger
Copyright © 2010 by Laura Manivong
www.harpercollinschildrens.com

Library of Congress Cataloging-in-Publication Data
Manivong, Laura, date
    Escaping the tiger / Laura Manivong. — 1st ed.
        p.   cm.
    Summary: In 1982, twelve-year-old Vonlai, his parents, and sister, Dalah, escape from Laos to a Thai refugee camp, where they spend four long years struggling to survive in hopes of one day reaching America.
    ISBN 978-0-06-166177-8
    [1. Refugees—Fiction. 2. Laotians—Thailand—Fiction. 3. Emigration and immigration—Fiction. 4. Brothers and sisters—Fiction. 5. Family life—Thailand—Fiction. 6. Laos—Politics and government—1975—Fiction. 7. Thailand—History—20th century—Fiction.]   I. Title.
PZ7.M31278Esc 2010   2009024095
[Fic]—dc22   CIP
                                                                                    AC

Typography by Larissa Lawrynenko

10 11 12 13 14   CG/RRDB   10 9 8 7 6 5 4 3 2 1
❖
First Edition

For Troy, Clara, and Aidan

"I can be changed by what happens to me.
But I refuse to be reduced by it."
—Maya Angelou
Words of Hope and Courage

Chapter
1

Vientiane, Laos, April 1982

Vonlai's father roused him in the middle of a moonless night.

"What? Stop it," Vonlai mumbled.

"*Shhh*. Wake up," Pah said, pulling Vonlai's elbow. "We're crossing tonight."

Vonlai wobbled on weary legs. Pah strapped a bag of beef jerky and sticky rice around Vonlai's shoulders. A shudder shot down Vonlai's neck and his mind snapped awake.

Vonlai's older sister, Dalah, was awake, too, teetering as she sat upright on the mattress, grumbling at their mother. Meh pulled Dalah's hair back, twisted two strands, and tied them into a knot.

"Ouch, Meh!" Dalah pulled on her hair to readjust it. "It's crooked."

"Who will see you?" Vonlai asked.

Meh snapped her fingers to quiet them and grunted her disapproval. "Surely you don't expect to be admired, girl. Now clear your mind and dress." Meh's voice cracked. "Without another word."

Vonlai steadied his tired body against the wall. He wouldn't add to Meh's worry by complaining.

Pah looked out the window, his hand on the doorknob. "Walk like a tiger hunting a meal. Understand?"

Vonlai's breath wavered as he nodded. He wanted to dive under his bedcovering, even though the night air was sticky and plenty warm. He held nothing but a pair of worn flip-flops hooked through his fingers and a day's worth of food—he needed to hold on to his nerve. Maybe his parents would see he was more grown up than other twelve-year-olds.

Pah turned the handle and walked out as confidently as if he were headed to the market. Meh stood in the doorway, knees locked. Vonlai pulled her hand. They all followed Pah out and slipped into the night. Most border patrol guards were teenagers accustomed to farming during daylight hours. They were likely to doze off under a black sky.

Vonlai knew the way to the Mekong River well, but last season's monsoon rains had turned the path into a maze of ankle-deep ruts. They'd dried cement hard, and with exposed tree roots, night travel was treacherous. Even with bare feet, Vonlai was uncertain of his footing. A knot in his throat swelled. His heart beat so hard, Vonlai was sure the guards could hear it.

Barely able to see, Vonlai concentrated to hear Pah's footsteps. It was the only way to keep track of him, but even that slight rustle over leaves and gravel unnerved him. Vonlai rounded his shoulders, humpbacked like an old man, as if stooped posture could make their escape impossible to detect.

The descent to the Mekong steepened. His feet shuffled to keep his body upright on the embankment. Vonlai tensed at the noise he created. A branch snagged his ankle. He stumbled and caught himself on a fallen tree, but not before his shin scraped the bark.

The bulk of gray that was his father did not pause. Vonlai waited for the soothing sound of Meh's voice, asking if he was all right. It didn't come.

A warm trickle oozed down his leg. Vonlai bent to wipe the blood. Dalah smacked his shoulder with her flip-flop. The sound shot through the night, the river echoing her impatience. How could she be so mindless to create such ruckus? Guards shoot at anything and don't think twice.

Vonlai breathed in fear, his lungs like clay. He forced his mind to think of happier times.

He'd raced down this river trail with friends nearly every day, the songs of fishermen floating up to greet them long before they could see the old men casting their nets. The last friend down got pelted with mud balls, and they dunked one another to save themselves from the heat. Sitting on the bank, biting into fleshy mangoes, they'd wondered about the tiny figures on the other side of the Mekong going so freely about their business. Thai citizens could do as they pleased. Vonlai and his friends had to hide secret pleasures, stifling giggles in back bedrooms as airwaves delivered forbidden TV programs. Silly game shows on Thai TV. Monstrous, white wrestlers in America, oiled and screaming, veins popping as crowds went wild.

Vonlai ducked fast, narrowly missing a tree limb. Dread flooded his heart. The war had ended seven years before, in 1975. Vonlai was not quite six then, so life under Communist control—the Pathet Lao—was all he remembered, but there were terrifying reminders to heed the rules. He and his friends once saw what they thought was the carcass of a buffalo calf coming downriver. They'd stood waist deep in the water as it drifted toward them, splashing to shoo it away.

"It's a body!" Vonlai had yelled. They scurried to land. "Ooh, look at it!"

A man floating faceup. Shirt buttons strained against

4

the bloated torso—exposed skin chalky, even translucent, like a frog's belly.

"It's gonna get stuck." His friend Sery grabbed a long stick and leaned close, careful to keep his feet out of the water.

"Leave it alone," Vonlai said, knocking away the stick. "You'll get us in trouble."

They all knew what had happened. The man tried to flee and was shot by Pathet Lao guards who dared not let anyone escape Laos—the same guards Vonlai and his family now tried to sneak past.

Pah and Meh dragged a tattered canoe from under a pile of brush. They eased it into the river. Vonlai and Dalah sat on the middle benches. Meh kept watch from the front, and Pah steered from the rear.

Out from under the canopy of trees, Vonlai's eyes adjusted. The sky enveloped them as starlight speckled the water's smooth surface.

Pah maneuvered the boat steadily until the current snatched hold of it.

Vonlai gripped the sides, and the Mekong took charge. He buried his head between his knees. *Why, of all nights,* he wondered, *could there not be a blanket of fog to screen my family from murdering eyes?*

He counted silently to busy his frenzied brain. How high would he get before the boat scraped bottom on the

Thai side? He tapped his feet with each new number.

97—*tap.*

98—*tap.*

99—*tap.*

Water splashed his shins. Water? Too much water. More than the bit that dripped from their feet after Pah pushed off.

Vonlai leaned toward Meh to whisper, "There's water in the boat."

Meh stretched her arm back. She laid her hand at Vonlai's feet. Water pooled over her wrist. "*Oi,* have mercy."

"I'll get the bowl," Vonlai said, feeling along the canoe's floor. The plastic bowl floated in the puddle. He handed it to Meh and with one smooth swoop after another, she bailed out the boat.

But the water kept coming. Pah paddled faster.

"Help me," Meh whispered. "Quietly!"

Vonlai searched for something to hold water. Their bamboo sticky rice basket, the color of light sand, stood out among the pile of dark canvas bags. Vonlai grabbed it. The lid was nested over the container, but Vonlai pulled the sections apart, breaking the string that kept them attached. He dumped the rice into the river and gave the basket to Dalah. Vonlai used the lid, and together they bailed water as fast as they could.

Meh kept a rhythm with her bowl as she whispered, "Scoop. Scoop. Scoop."

"That's it," Pah said as water swirled and gushed around his oars. "We need out of this current."

Vonlai's arms burned. Dalah whimpered.

The river was winning. They were only halfway across, but the shores of Thailand were still black as tar.

"Faster," Meh commanded.

Scoop. Scoop. Scoop.

Dalah threw down the basket and wrapped her arms around her shoulders. "We're not going to make it!"

Vonlai screamed at her inside his head—*shut up, shut up*—and froze as he waited for the bullet.

Pah's oars smacked the Mekong, shattering the hushed river.

Crack! Crack! Crack! Bullets from AK-47s pierced the wall of darkness surrounding them.

Dalah screamed.

"Quiet, daughter!" Meh said. "We're invisible if they can't hear us."

Pah repositioned his oars for smoother strokes.

"Bail, Dalah. Please," Vonlai whispered.

Crack! Crack!

Dalah grabbed her sticky rice container again. Water flew everywhere. Vonlai's blood raged, same as a swollen stream thrashing its banks after monsoons. He tried to steady his breaths, a rhythm to temper their frenzied efforts.

It seemed that they were making progress, but Vonlai couldn't be sure. And he dared not ask. He searched for signs, shadows that would outline the bank. Were those trees he saw, great gray masses that blocked the backdrop of stars? He judged their distance. Maybe a soccer field's length to go.

Pah's paddling slowed.

"Good. Good," Pah said between pants. "Very good. We should be out of range now."

Vonlai heard water lapping the banks of Thailand. Yes, his eyes had not tricked him. They were close now.

Scoop. Scoop. Scoop. Then *SNAP!* Meh's plastic bowl cracked.

The river had no mercy. Water came twice as fast without Meh's efforts. Vonlai was wet halfway to his knees. He tossed his half of the rice basket to Meh. She was stronger. Vonlai cupped his hands to scoop. Meh whacked at the water, cursing under her breath. Dalah's arms buckled. She gave up and kicked at the rising pool. "We're sinking, Meh!"

"Come on, daughter," Pah said, passing an oar to Meh. "Show us your strength." Dalah slumped over her lap, shaking her arms to divert the pain. Pah and Meh paddled in unison, leaning their weight into the oars. Vonlai plucked the sticky rice lid floating in the canoe and bailed again.

Meh glanced back at Pah. "My arms won't hold out. We have to swim."

"Too soon," Pah said. "The current will swallow us. Switch arms."

The river carried them downstream. Pah and Meh angled the canoe toward shore.

Dalah latched on to her basket with both hands, but her arms were drained. Feathers would have been no easier to heave over the edge. "Curse the dogs who sold us this shabby boat!" she said, crying.

"Use that anger on the Mekong," Meh said.

Vonlai was past pain. His pace wasn't even half of Meh's, his arms numb, his fingers barely holding a grip. The bamboo lid bulged. The rim was shredded. He dropped it nearly as often as he scooped.

They managed a few more meters before Vonlai collapsed against the boat's side. Dalah was barely upright, one arm cradled in her lap, the other hanging over the edge, trailing like a fish on a line.

"The current's weaker," Meh said. "It must be now— we've only got our legs left."

Pah nodded.

Vonlai sucked in a breath as Pah laid down his oar and lowered himself into the water. Meh followed.

The sight of them in the river sent Vonlai's stomach roiling. What if Pah and Meh lost hold of the boat? He and

Dalah would be carried right into the barrel of an AK-47 and his parents would drown—or the Mekong's giant catfish, big as baby elephants, would gnash into them.

"Come on," Pah said.

Vonlai stood up fast and grabbed the edge.

"Easy," Meh said.

Vonlai and Dalah tried to get out at the same time. The canoe tilted under their weight. Water gushed over the edge. Instantly the boat was full. Dalah thrashed and kicked.

Pah grabbed her ponytail. "Hang on to the boat!" he commanded. "We have to flip it!"

Even a weak current could be deadly. The canoe was their lifeline.

Everyone held the boat's edge. Meh gripped Vonlai's shirt.

"On three," Pah said. "One! Two! Three!" They pushed their weight on the edge. The canoe flipped fast. It smacked Meh's chin. She moaned and lost her grip on Vonlai. He slipped away under the cool Mekong water.

His shirt billowed as the dark water pulled him along. Vonlai searched for something to hold. *Which way was up?* he wondered. Black surrounded him. Water rushed down his throat like a serrated knife. He pushed and thrashed and scraped against the force heavy as quicksand. Demons plunged their claws into his lungs and pierced his brain.

Muffled voices called out. "Vonlaiii! Vonlaiii!"

Ghosts, he thought, *pulling me toward death.* His leg brushed something solid. *Another rotting corpse,* his mind conjured up. It latched on to his ankle and pulled violently. Vonlai returned a kick with his free leg, but it was too late. The Thing had an unbreakable grip and forced his body up with its power. Vonlai was at its mercy.

Then air! Sputtering—coughing—spitting. But air!

Vonlai gasped as he clung to Pah's neck.

"Swim, Vonlai. Now! We lost the boat!"

Vonlai refused to let go.

"Meh and Dalah couldn't wait," Pah said. "Now go! Buddha can't save you!"

Vonlai had never heard Pah doubt Buddha. The shock of it jump-started his body, and he fought his way toward land. The current pulled him so he swam at an angle, flipping on his back to use new muscles. He'd lost track of Pah, but he pushed on.

One stroke after another.

One breath after another.

One wave of hope after another.

Underwater plants brushed his back. His feet hit mud. Vonlai dragged himself onto the banks of Thailand.

He lay panting facedown in the sludge, alone, and gulped mouthfuls of air. His stomach rolled and he turned his head to throw up.

Meh and Dalah called to him from the brush. He had

no voice to answer, and his body refused to move.

He heard the shriek of an unfamiliar bird and thought dawn must be near, but there was not yet a sliver of light to separate sky from earth. The shriek came again, and he felt it in his throat. The wailing was his own voice crying out.

His mother cradled his head, and Dalah threw her body down next to him, her arm draped over his back.

"Oh, Little Brother, if you'd died, I'd throw myself in the river. I should have tried harder—" Her words turned to sobs.

Pah stumbled along the shoreline to meet them, collapsing in the sand. "They can't get us here, Vonlai. We're on Thai soil now."

Thailand. Not Laos, the only place he'd ever known. They'd escaped that home, abandoned their house, leaving behind the few possessions that hadn't been taken by the Pathet Lao—or sold off in order to eat. A single-coil cook plate, dented pots, a cane table with one leg missing, and bowed metal chairs. And Vonlai's bike. His bike that had a rolled towel wired and taped on for a seat.

Vonlai thought of his best friend, Khom, still sleeping on the other side of the Mekong under Communist rule. In a couple hours, the roosters would crow their alarm. Khom would rattle Vonlai's front door with soccer ball in one hand and slingshot in the other.

Vonlai never said good-bye.

Chapter
2

Northeastern Thailand

Makeshift light poles lined the bank. They marked foot-paths that served as docks to those living along the Mekong. The fluorescent tubes hung vertically on short posts like swords drawn for battle. Their dim glow hummed as insects flitted around.

"Look for the purple light," Pah said, walking along the riverbank.

"We're too far downstream," Meh said. She heaved Vonlai up, his body squelching out of the mud.

Dalah wiped globs of silt off his chest. "What purple light are you talking about, Pah?"

"We arranged for a man to help us. He marked his dock," Pah said. "Now quiet yourself."

A violet glow lit the eastern horizon. Birds chattered

on the Thai side of the river the same as if Vonlai were lying in his bed in Laos, letting the day arrive slowly. He longed for that familiar comfort.

"Here," a voice called. "Come along now."

"You must be Virasack," Pah said as a man appeared, wearing only shorts and flip-flops.

"Is everyone here? I heard shots."

"Yes, Brother," Pah said. "We are blessed. And forever in your debt."

The man pointed up a path. "This way. Please."

Vonlai and his family made their way through the brush toward the row of river houses built on stilts. An old woman approached, laboring toward the water with a basket of clothes. "Hmmpf. Filthy dog faces. We have nothing for you here."

Vonlai knew he was the target of her harsh tongue. Mud caked his body, and he certainly looked like a beggar. He swallowed the anger, bitter and bleeding in his throat, but the shame showed on him, red across his cheeks, like a stripe of paint marking a forbidden act.

"She has many burdens," Virasack said. "Doesn't take kindly to Lao in her land looking for a better life when her days are filled with struggle. Now come inside. Please. So I don't lose the goodwill of more neighbors."

As Vonlai followed his parents up to the man's house, the sun lit treetops in the distance. He saw across the

Mekong to Laos, where he knew border patrol guards had tried to kill him. And now his heart throbbed knowing people here hated him, too, not for anything he did, but because of where he was born.

Vonlai's foot landed on a sharp edge, and he cried out.

"We'll tend to that inside, boy," the man said. "For now, hold your tongue."

Vonlai sank his foot in the cool earth to stop the burn.

Virasack paused at the stairs outside his house. Meh and Pah cleaned their feet with water from the bathing barrel and followed the man inside. Dalah tried to help Vonlai rinse out his shirt.

"I can do it," he said, scooping a bowlful of water to pour down his chest.

"You scared?" Dalah asked, watching him shiver.

"That woman hates us for nothing."

"Take off your shirt." Dalah handed Vonlai a towel. "We can wring it out better."

Inside the house, the man had a bed of blankets ready for them on the floor. Vonlai and Dalah rested on the mound while a woman offered cups of water. *Doesn't she know how much of the Mekong I've already swallowed?* Vonlai wondered. But there was kindness in her eyes. Vonlai was ashamed to feel anger toward a woman offering help. He took the cup from her outstretched hand.

Two boys sat on the floor at the edge of the room, sleepy-eyed but staring. They looked a few years older than Vonlai, about the same age as the Communist guards watching the Lao border. Vonlai wanted nothing more than to curl up and let sleep wash away the past few hours. He wanted a dream to take him back home, where he had friends and clothes and secret hideaways, but too many questions unnerved him. Did these boys hate Vonlai's family the same as the old woman did? Did they wonder how different their lives might be if fate had switched their birthplace? Maybe they were too content to burden themselves with any thought other than returning to sleep.

"I see you lost everything in the river," Virasack said.

"As long as we don't die, we can find possessions again," Pah said.

Vonlai examined his foot. Sand peppered the cut. No one in his family even had a pair of rubber flip-flops. But he'd been told to hold his tongue.

"We have some meager supplies to offer," Virasack said. "And we'll get that wound clean for you, boy."

The woman pulled a box from under the kitchen table. Tattered pots and blankets filled it. She laid four pairs of flip-flops on top. They were all the same size, way too big for Vonlai. His foot began to throb, and he could feel Dalah shiver next to him. The woman kept the box close to her.

"Tomorrow," the man continued, "my cousin will show you to the Nong Khai police station. You'll stay there for processing until your group gains entry to the refugee camp. It could be a months-long wait. And the conditions are far from pleasant."

"We have money, even American dollars." Pah looked to Meh for reassurance.

"Yes, we still have it," Meh said, pulling out the pouch hidden in her bra.

"Good," Virasack said. "You can bribe your way onto a bus sooner and pray your time in Na Pho will be swift."

Vonlai was eager to get out of his wet clothes. The woman caught his gaze and handed him a T-shirt from the box, tattered but about his size. Meh offered her a few loose bills. The woman accepted them, and Meh put her hands together in the traditional prayer gesture to show her thanks.

The woman tucked the money in her skirt and went to the kitchen. She returned with a tray of sticky rice, chicken broth, and sliced cucumbers. She set it on a bamboo mat spread on the floor in front of them.

As the smell awakened his hunger, Vonlai realized even kindness came at a price, and he was glad his parents had money to pay for it.

Chapter
3

Virasack's cousin Tanh came at midday.

"Let's load up," he said, nudging Dalah with his foot. "There'll be plenty of time to sleep away the day in Nong Khai, but you have to hurry and get there so the waiting can begin."

Meh and Pah were awake and packing. They stuffed the goods they'd bought from Virasack's wife into bags and double-checked their documents.

Dalah rolled over and swung her arm at the man's leg. She shot upright and glared at him as if still engaged in a dream-inspired battle.

"Eh, that's a feisty one," the man said to Pah.

"A lazy one, too," Vonlai whispered as he pushed her off the bedding so he could get up.

At midday, the Mekong was brimming with activity. Children splashed in the muddy water while women scrubbed clothes and rinsed dishes. Dogs trolled along the bank yipping and kicking up mud as they sniffed for scraps.

Vonlai's family followed Tanh inland for twenty minutes. Tanh waved his hand and hailed a tuk-tuk, a three-wheeled motorized rickshaw. Meh handed him money and Tanh passed it to the driver, leaning in to give instructions.

Tanh shook Pah's hand, while Vonlai and Dalah climbed onto the bench. "Good luck, friends. And remember, you might have escaped the tiger in Laos, but there are crocodiles in Nong Khai, so don't be too quick to pay off the police there. They'll delay your process to excess and drain your money."

Vonlai watched through the bars of the tuk-tuk as Thai citizens carried on with the day's tasks—ordinary tasks that wouldn't alter their lives drastically whether they were accomplished in any hurry or not—walking to the market, driving to work, chasing away hungry dogs. Scooters whizzed by loaded with passengers, the faces of toddlers especially carefree and bright as they peered over the handles from their spot between adults' legs.

The tuk-tuk stopped at the curb. Pah barely unloaded the bags before the driver pulled away. Vonlai stared at the building. Government offices, including the police station, lined the upper level, but the bottom was open, a big floor flanked by pillars at each corner. The only walls were sheets of cardboard and corrugated tin, rigged up by refugees—more than a hundred of them—trying to claim a space as their own. Bedrolls, clothes, water bottles, and shoes littered the floor. The smell of urine and sweat hung in the air, lingering under the concrete canopy.

"Go, go, go!" a Thai policeman said as he nudged Pah's back toward a line of tables along the wall. "There isn't time to gawk, you Lao dogs. Move it so you can get signed in."

"Go find us a space," Pah told Meh as he pushed Vonlai and Dalah out of the way. He leaned over the table to fill out papers to apply for refugee status.

"How about over there?" Vonlai said, pointing to an area near a stack of warped boxes.

Meh stepped over bodies to check if anyone else had reserved that spot. She waved Vonlai and Dalah over. "Sit here," she said as she threw down their bags.

Wet stink soaked through the bottom of the boxes. Flies buzzed around the seepage.

Dalah folded her arms across her chest. "It's filthy," she said. "And that's barely enough room for two of us."

"It's where you'll bed down. There's no other space. Now sit. Before someone else takes it and you have to sleep standing up."

That evening, a dinner line formed along the back

wall. "Chow time," Vonlai said. "Let's go. I'm starved."

"Ugh," Dalah said, wrinkling her nose. "That food smells worse than the pee on the floor."

"So hold your nose. I'm eating."

After waiting an hour in line, Vonlai sat on his bedroll, staring into his cup of stale, watery rice. "Is there even any meat in there?"

"It's tuna," Meh said.

"Must be the ghost of tuna, because I can't see it," Vonlai said, swirling his cup.

"Smell it. You can tell," Dalah said. "They must have spared a whole can to feed a dozen of us. Reeks as bad as your underarms."

Vonlai lifted the sleeve of his T-shirt to flex a muscle at Dalah. "That's my manly smell."

Dalah smiled a bit and her face relaxed. "Put that away before someone mistakes your arm for a chopstick."

"Shush and eat so you can sleep," Pah said, downing his slop in one gulp.

Vonlai tipped his cup and forced a swallow. Something flew past him, and a boy, a teenager, jumped over him and gave it chase. It was a ball. Not a real one, just balled-up socks, almost as big as a genuine soccer ball.

Vonlai stood, leaning around a building pillar to see a group of boys gathering to play. They made a racket with their yelling and kicked up dust as they faced off. Any one of those boys could have been Khom, ready to shoot the ball his way and run with him toward the goal.

Vonlai could barely keep his feet still. "Pah, can I go play?"

"You shouldn't go," Dalah said. "Those boys will trounce you. They're twice your size."

"But half as fast, I bet," Vonlai said.

"Not a good idea." Pah didn't look up. "See those guards there?"

A group of three men, rifles resting on their shoulders, laughed among themselves and passed around a cup.

"I see them," Vonlai said. "They're not paying any attention."

"They're always paying attention," Pah said. "And that's not water they're sharing."

"Are they drunk?" Dalah asked.

Meh rolled up their clothes and repacked a duffel bag. "Stay clear of them. And stop staring."

Vonlai tried to ignore the sounds of the game, the feet pounding across packed dirt, the calls to pass the ball, the congratulatory slapping of hands. It sounded too much like home.

He focused on an old woman with a stooped back who arranged her blanket on the floor. Her fingers were crooked, but she took care to get her bedding straight and smooth. She lay down on her side, her knees and elbows jutting nearly through her skin.

Just then, the ball shot over the woman's head, hit a wall, and rolled into a baby sleeping on the floor. The infant roared, and a tall boy, maybe Dalah's age, rushed through the crowd to retrieve the ball. He stumbled over bags and trampled across the edge of the old woman's blanket, leaving a trail of dusty footprints as he scooped up the ball.

"Curses, you fool!" the woman yelled, crouching on her knees to begin the straightening process again.

The boy was ready to dropkick the ball back to his team when a guard rammed his rifle into the back of the boy's knees. He fell awkwardly and lay curled on the ground crying.

Vonlai moved closer to see. The other guards had corralled the players into a huddle while the boy moaned in the dirt. "That's enough racket, you stinking mutt," the guard yelled, and he brought the rifle down between the boy's shoulder blades, a sick thud shooting through the hushed onlookers. The boy's body went limp.

Vonlai felt a hand on his back and he winced with imagined pain.

"Come away, Little Brother," Dalah whispered. "You shouldn't be here."

A woman rushed to the boy but was pushed to the ground by a guard. "When your son gets up, teach him respect, or I'll do it for you. Understand?"

The woman nodded nervously, wiping tears with one hand and reaching out to her son with the other.

Vonlai let Dalah usher him back to their spot. He laid out his bedroll and tried to sleep, but the forced silence wracked his nerves.

It was barely conceivable that the night before last, he'd been in his own house in Laos, lying on the tattered mattress he shared with Dalah, thinking he'd wake up to the same routine. Now confusion clogged his thinking. The uncertainty of the future was a weight on his chest, and his breath ratcheted in and out.

Over the past weeks he'd listened late at night as his parents whispered in the dark. If they'd known he was awake, they would never have spoken the words—the sour thoughts that built up on the back of the tongue like pus—that, once spat out, could cost people their lives.

"Vientiane City will not recover," Pah had said, his feet padding the floor as he paced around their house. He tried to maintain a soft voice. "It's rotting under Communist lies and we can say nothing. Nothing! My mind breaks every day as I try to keep my mouth shut. And the neighbors? I don't know who's a spy and who isn't—what if my tongue slips? They'd whisk us away to seminar camp. Shove more Marxist doctrine down our throats. Work us to death bit by bit so the world cannot call them killers."

"But didn't you hear what Vonlai's teacher said?" Meh

asked. "He has family in Thailand. Those refugee camps are dangerous, too. People are desperate. They turn against each other. And how many have already been killed crossing the Mekong?"

"More people die now by staying! And we're hypocrites to have to pretend the Pathet Lao is our friend. They *are* the enemy—there, I said it out loud."

Pah had released a long sigh and dragged a chair across the floor, the familiar creak of rusted metal crying out as he sat down. His voice was winded from his rant. Vonlai pulled a sheet over his head, but he could still hear.

"Yes, their words sounded good at first, but they've tricked us all these years. Empty promises, that's all. There *is* no economic equality. No religious freedom." Pah slammed a fist into his palm as he spoke. "And now we're watching our children starve!"

"Shush," Meh said. "You'll wake them."

"They'll know soon enough. Even the Pathet Lao pawns can't feed their families anymore and it's been seven years since the war. Seven years and nothing is better! If the Communists are deserting, what chance do we have for better lives? We have to go. And soon. Before the refugee camps stop admitting civilians."

Vonlai had never allowed himself to believe the day would come when it was time to leave Laos. He never imagined what lay beyond the trek across the Mekong, but there he was, lying on the rock-hard floor underneath a Thai police station, waiting for the unknown.

The days dragged on in Nong Khai. Refugees passed the time in front of the police station in the heat, squatting in a bit of shade to smoke cigarettes, play cards, and read old magazines and weathered comic books. If anyone wandered too far, guards prodded them back like wayward buffalo. "We can't have you filthy dogs escaping into Thai countryside. Stay put."

After a week, UNHCR—the United Nations High Commissioner for Refugees—began to process application papers. Shards of excitement veined out from Vonlai's heart as he saw the officials set up their processing station on a table.

A Thai policeman held up his hand. "If you hear your name, line up for interviews." He started reading. *Please call us,* Vonlai prayed. He dug his fingernails into his palms as the policeman's eyes scanned the list.

Another policeman patrolled the line. "Make sure your documents are in order. If not, you'll be sent back without making an application."

Vonlai's family was not called. He chewed the inside of his cheek to hold his tongue, but longing and frustration swirled inside him and he thought he might burst. "Pah, is that it? Can't you go double-check?"

"Quiet. Creating an irritation for the police will not

help our cause. Now sit back."

They watched as the line snaked out from the tables and past their resting spot. Children clung to parents' knees, wailing to be entertained, as the line crept along. A policeman approached a man who'd been waiting near them.

"Did you make sure your documents are in order? *All* your documents?" the policeman asked, standing too close to the man's face.

"Yes, everything's here." The man showed his papers.

"Hmmm," the policeman said, flipping through the stack too fast to read anything. "It doesn't appear that way to me." He pulled the man out of line. "Maybe your name will get called again next week. Maybe not."

Vonlai wanted Pah to jump up and trade places with the man—to shove money in the hands of the police. Anything to get out, but Pah stayed put, leaning against his bedroll and appearing disinterested. He was heeding Tanh's warning to exercise patience when bribing an official. Vonlai kept his eyes averted so as not to attract the policeman's attention, but he kept his ears wide open.

"Oh, sir. You're right," the man said. "There is one more document. If I could beg your patience." Vonlai couldn't help but look. He saw the man reach down into his bag and fold money into a piece of paper. Then he slipped it onto the stack the policeman held.

The policeman peeked into the folded paper. "My

mistake," he said as he slid the money in his pocket. "It seems you do have your papers in order after all. Now move along. You're holding up the line."

After nearly a month in Nong Khai dodging the police, Vonlai's family got their turn. Pah paid off a policeman, and they presented their documents to the UNHCR. They were processed and approved to enter Na Pho refugee camp, based on economic hardship.

A group of more than fifty Lao waited outside. Children, hungry and crying from a missed breakfast, sat in the dirt next to their parents, who were too exhausted to comfort them. The bus arrived after two hours, and the group elbowed its way in. Children piled on their parents' laps to make room for all the passengers.

As the bus pulled away, Vonlai felt a prickling of relief as the blood that ran icy through his veins began to warm up. *Such a relief to be going somewhere*, Vonlai thought, *away from this awful place where people called us dogs just for being Lao.* He settled in for the daylong trek across Thai countryside. His eyelids grew heavy as the bus rumbled on.

With bags stacked and bulging on top of the bus, it serpentined its way along curved roads. A man standing to stretch lost his balance and landed on Vonlai. Vonlai shot awake and rubbed his eyes. People lay in the aisle and under the seats asleep.

Vonlai stared out the back of the bus. A haze of dust rose behind the tires, but he looked past it. He watched the road they'd traveled wind down from the green mountains and shrink in the distance. He had never been so far away from home. The landscape was still beautiful through the grime on the bus windows.

The valley was lush and wide open. The rains had come early this year, and farmers laden with bulging baskets of rice plants went about their work. They walked backward in a crouch, reaching through ankle-deep water to plug seedlings into the soil.

Vonlai lost count of the hours his family had been on the bus, packed in among the sweaty, bobbling bodies. He'd missed two meals that day, but the grit in his teeth destroyed any appetite he might have had.

Worry about food had not yet entered his thoughts, but the life he left behind did.

"Meh, what about schoolwork?" Vonlai asked.

Pah was asleep and Dalah sat quiet, crammed under a window with bodies reaching over her for fresh air. She pushed an arm out of her way and sat up. "Forget about school," she snapped. "Don't you get it? We're refugees now." She glared at Meh. "We don't *have* a school anymore, or a house, or friends."

Meh laid her head against the seat back and closed her eyes to the world. She couldn't see the tears that left streaks of regret on Dalah's face.

Vonlai thought back to their last night in Laos and wondered why Pah had even bothered to help him study for a math exam. Life had felt so normal, so routine, but what was the point?

Vonlai's mind returned to the farmers focused on their tasks in the rice fields. Could they sense the sadness and fear that seeped from the bus sputtering through their fields? Maybe. But what could they do? The world was crumbling around them, and there was work to be done. Always work to be done. It was *their* routine. Besides, what help was a rice farmer to a busload of unwanted refugees, anyway?

Chapter
4

Na Pho Refugee Camp, Thailand, May 1982

The metal gate slammed behind Vonlai. The rattle shot through him like a jolt of electricity, and he shivered despite the heat. A guard threaded a chain through the gate and snapped the padlock.

Children leaned against parents, listless from the dust that coated them chalky brown, the luster of black hair lost under a layer of grit.

It's not right, Vonlai thought. *Those little kids—so lazy-acting. Back home, kids that age were pests, always swinging from trees, flustering the chickens, sword fighting with strips of bamboo. What kind of place is this?*

Maybe it's the heat, Vonlai told himself. *There's no river. No relief.* His own back was dripping, his shirt soaked through with sweat where his duffel bag of mismatched clothes lay against him.

They passed long buildings with packed dirt porches. The sheet-metal roofs, lined with veins of rust, reflected heat that warped the sky. Vonlai remembered the house he left in Laos. The clean white driveway that stretched to the road, long and flat and smooth. He and Khom had practiced soccer kicks against his concrete house every day after school. Did someone else live there now? Were rats sleeping in his bed, fat and fearless after gorging on grains of abandoned rice? Had Khom forgotten him already?

Vonlai followed Pah and the guard to the refugee-processing building. He tucked his head down to keep the stench of stagnant water out of his nostrils. Dalah walked with a mosquito net draped around her shoulders, and Meh carried the bag of cooking pots they'd bought from the family on the Mekong. It bobbled against her hip with each step. The clatter stirred Vonlai's hunger. It was almost dusk, and he'd yet to eat. He could no longer ignore the emptiness that gnawed at him.

Inside the building, Vonlai tried to sit upright on the bench that lined the wall. Pah and Meh filled out paperwork. Dalah slouched over her own lap, her face buried behind a wall of hair that should have been washed a week ago. An oscillating fan pushed a blanket of air toward them every few seconds.

"This place stinks," Dalah said, her voice muffled in her lap.

Vonlai swept palmfuls of sweat from behind his knees. "Pah said we shouldn't be here long. We'll get our papers soon."

"Did you see those people outside?" Dalah asked. "They don't look like they've been here a short time. They're skinnier than you."

Vonlai rubbed a hand across his leg. A streak of clean skin appeared and a muddy drip of sweat fell from his hand. His thighs were barely wider than his kneecaps now. After more than three weeks in Nong Khai getting by on slivers of tuna and rice, his stomach screamed for food, but he wasn't sure he had the energy to eat anything.

Vonlai closed his eyes. He tried to hang on to the words Pah had spoken all those long nights on the hard police station floor. Whispers of living in a free country like France or maybe America, where Pah's second cousin had gone, a place where Vonlai and Dalah would have a brand-new school. Their own desks. Fat books. New friends. A new life.

Pah rolled up their documents and tapped Vonlai's shoulder. "We received our building assignment," he said, stashing the papers in his bag. "Let's find it before dark."

Wire fencing surrounded the camp. Plastic bags, tangled in the barbs, flapped like birds with clipped wings.

They found their building and peeked inside.

"This is where we'll live?" Vonlai asked as they walked under the overhang and entered their room. There was not a single chair or table on the hard-packed dirt floor. Only four hooks in the ceiling over each corner of one bamboo bed—a wide bed designed to sleep a whole family like sardines in a can. The corrugated metal wall served as a headboard, the other three sides were exposed. Meh pulled the mosquito net from Dalah's shoulders and stood on the bed to attach it.

"Don't we get a sheet?" asked Dalah. "Or pillows?"

"Roll up a shirt and tuck it in your bag," Meh answered.

"One bed for all of us?" Vonlai asked.

Pah nodded.

"If you kick me just one time," Dalah warned, "I'll roll you right into the dirt."

"Stop it!" Meh said. Her arms quivered as she tried to attach the net. "Do you think complaining will change your fate? It won't—this is it. Now our rations are coming soon, and unless you want to eat hard grains of rice, we need to get to the water station before they close it for the night."

Dalah climbed atop the bed and took the net from Meh's hands. She reached the hooks with no problem.

"Hmpf," Meh said. "Taller than me already. And

with a mouth to match."

Outside the barracks, a cluster of refugees sat under a lone tree like buffalo in a field, huddling their hot bodies together to share the spot of shade. Old men, cigarettes clenched in their lips and eyes squinted to keep out the smoke, sliced bamboo into long strips to weave rice baskets. A crowd of boys passed around a bottle of orange Fanta, each one threatening the next if he dared to swallow more than a sip. Women squatted around the common cooking areas, feet flat on the ground and knees against their chests, pounding their pestles into clay-fired mortars while rice steamed over open fires. Still others fanned themselves and stared into the dirt.

Meh dumped their bag of goods onto the bed and found a pot. A man stopped by to drop off a meal's worth of rice. Vonlai stared at his name tag. It was dark green with white letters—English letters.

"What does it say?" Vonlai asked.

Meh stiffened, her demure smile an attempt to offset Vonlai's boldness.

"My name: Keng," he answered. "And here . . ."—Keng ran a finger over each of the words and said them in English—"*Joint. Volunteer. Agency.* We work under the UNHCR to process those going to America."

Vonlai took a step to get a closer look at the letters. "You can read that?"

"I suppose so. Otherwise, I could have said my name is Superman."

"Ha—I saw a Superman comic book when we were in Thailand waiting to come here," Vonlai said. "Looks like you forgot your red cape."

"Child!" Meh said. "Go fold our clothes and make yourself less of a nuisance." She turned to the man. "Thank you, sir. You were kind to get this to us this evening."

Pah came back with an armload of wood. He stacked it in the cooking pit while Dalah and Meh picked stones out of the rice for their first dinner in Na Pho.

That night, Vonlai lay awake next to Pah, whose snoring seemed to vibrate the close quarters of the bed. Dalah slept next to Vonlai, with Meh finishing the line. "You awake, Meh?" he whispered.

She shifted her body but didn't answer. Vonlai's thoughts bounced around, searching for something to anticipate, but there was nothing. No friends to come knocking. No sandbar for burying calloused feet. No kip in his pocket, itching to be spent on bags of sugarcane juice to sip between soccer games.

He thought about the Lao man, Keng, who had brought their rice—his name written in English. Vonlai fantasized about the form his own name would take should he learn how to write it.

Dalah mumbled in her sleep, rolled over, and stretched her leg out against Vonlai's back. Her skin was sticky, so he scooted to the bottom edge of the bed. The bare bamboo pinched the back of his thigh, and he bit his lip to keep from crying out. He straightened his legs, his feet poking past the mosquito net and over the bed rail. The parasites wasted no time. Vonlai pulled his legs back in and scratched the growing welts on his toes.

He was hungry. For dinner, they'd each had a palmful of steamed rice, stale and tasteless. No meat. No vegetables. No nam jeel. He hadn't had pepper sauce in weeks. Just one dab of its fiery flavor would have been more welcomed than a double portion of rice.

Vonlai heard scuffling outside their barracks and wondered if a dog was looking for scraps to eat. *Nothing here, poor mutt,* Vonlai thought. *We've eaten every grain of rice.*

A shadow appeared next to the bed near his father, but it was too tall to be a dog's. Vonlai shifted to see better, and the shadow paused. It waited. It listened.

Vonlai couldn't speak. He couldn't move.

The figure crouched and rummaged through their bags.

Vonlai was paralyzed. His hand lay at the bed's top edge, the mosquito net brushing his skin. In seconds, a buzz of bloodsuckers slipped between the net and the wall, attacking through tiny holes in the mesh, feeding on that one accessible patch of skin.

The thief tossed their clothes onto the floor and dug deeper for something he couldn't find. *Doesn't he know I'm wide awake and watching him?* Vonlai wondered. He tried to close his eyes, but his body was rigid.

The shadow paused and stared at the bed, a pot clenched in its hand.

Can he see my open eyes? Is he going to slit my neck right here as I lie among my family?

A groan escaped Vonlai's throat. The crook stood up, clanking the pot against the bed rail. Pah shot straight up and pulled the net.

"Get out, fool!" Pah screamed. "The Communists already stole what we had."

The thief dropped his load and scampered away.

Everyone was awake now. Dalah was crying. She leaned her head into Meh's shoulder as Pah gathered up their clothes. Vonlai's heart scratched at the walls of his chest.

A raspy, weak voice called out to them from the doorway. "That scoundrel would be lucky to live his next life as a tick on a dog's rear."

The shadow that belonged to *this* voice was hunched and crooked. Dalah quieted to listen to the stranger.

"You won't be bothered again after news spreads that you have nothing to steal."

Vonlai could not tell if the figure was that of a man or a woman. The voice was so hoarse, it gave no clue. The stranger left as quickly as it had appeared. Maybe it was really a lost spirit unaware it was dead, still wandering between this world and the next. Vonlai shivered as it shuffled away with its lame foot.

Step. Scrape. Step. Scrape. Step. Scrape.

Vonlai rolled closer to Pah and lay his head back on the bed, grateful now that his family owned nothing of value.

Chapter
5

Vonlai opened his eyes to see a lizard perched in the corner of the ceiling. For one cruel moment, he thought he was late for school, but his stomach wasted no time reminding him where he was. He rolled over to abandon his sweat-soaked patch of bed and lay there examining his hand. He counted twenty-eight mosquito bites there alone, in the exact spot where his skin had rested against the net when the thief came in. Vonlai scratched until he drew blood.

Dalah and Meh spoke softly outside.

Vonlai sat up and looked at all four walls. The box of a room seemed smaller in full daylight.

"No more rice yet?" he asked from the doorway.

"Have a drink of water." Meh handed him a cup, her eyes avoiding his. Vonlai knew the answer. He gulped the water and left to relieve himself.

The latrines formed a row behind Vonlai's living

quarters. A block of ten toilets for all the families in his building—twenty at least, Vonlai guessed. More than a hundred people sharing ten toilets.

He tried not to breathe as he enclosed himself in the stall. Mosquitoes swarmed over the hole as he squatted. Slatted light seeped through the vent, but fresh air could not find its way in. The stench burned his nose. Mosquitoes attacked his bare backside. Vonlai bunched his pants as high as he could around his privates to protect himself until he could finish.

Outside, a truck rumbled past. Food, he hoped. His stomach felt no trace of last night's rice. He stepped out to see the rusty heap lurch to a stop. It plunged a long, plastic tube into a hole in the ground.

Vonlai watched as it siphoned out the latrine waste, stirring up the stink. Nausea swelled in his gut. He bent over and heaved, throwing up nothing but the water he'd just drunk.

Still doubled over and clutching his middle, Vonlai winced as a lit cigarette landed on his bare foot. He kicked it off and looked up. A Thai security guard laughed and blew a cloud of smoke in his face. Vonlai waited for him to say something, to give an instruction.

The man grinned, baring broken yellow teeth. "I saw your sister. She's real pretty. I bet when she fills out she'll be just as pretty as your mother."

Vonlai's right eye twitched, a bad sign. He held his tongue to be respectful, even though the guard spoke empty compliments. He didn't want his parents to get word of any misbehavior, but a man who threw fire on his foot and spoke double-talk was to be avoided.

Vonlai turned away from the guard, slowly at first, with careful steps. He heard the guard strike a match and draw on another cigarette.

Vonlai returned in a hurry to his barracks. He was on the lookout for any bad thing, a stubbed toe, a splinter—anything except another encounter with the guard—that could satisfy the omen of his twitching right eye.

"Where's Pah?" he asked Meh.

"He's gone to check on the rations and finish our entry documents. Dalah will show you where your school is."

"With no rice to eat?"

"You can't attend today, anyway. Just go see where it is—but don't be nosy. There'll be rice for dinner." Meh looked unconvinced. "Stay together. I've already shown Dalah the way."

"What will you do, Meh?" Dalah asked.

"I'll start breaking up the dirt for a garden. We're due some vegetable seeds."

Seeds, not vegetables, Vonlai thought. *Will we have to grow our own food in order to get a full meal?*

Vonlai and Dalah walked toward the center of camp,

past barrack after barrack.

"A mango tree," Vonlai yelled, pointing beyond the latrines. They raced toward it and stood panting under its branches. He grabbed a low limb and pulled himself into the canopy of leaves, rustling the branches overhead.

"Toss them down!" Dalah called.

"There's hardly any left."

"Hey, you rats!" A young woman with a baby at her breast threatened them with a wooden spoon. "Get away from my tree!"

"*Your* tree?" Vonlai asked. His face flushed at the shock of hearing the rudeness in his voice.

"My barracks." The woman pounded the spoon on the wall. "My tree."

Vonlai jumped off the branch and backed off. A dog came sniffing at the woman's rice pot. As she turned to smack the scavenger, Vonlai snatched a mango and pulled Dalah's arm toward the footpath. They ran around the side of a building and leaned against the wall, the baby's cries following them down the alley.

Vonlai bit into the juicy fruit and handed it to Dalah. She hesitated, her eyes eager, then took a small bite and gave it back. "You finish it," Dalah said. "You need it more than me."

"But I'm ashamed. I stole from her."

"It's not her tree. She's a refugee just like us. And we're

43

hungry just like her."

"Then you have to share it with me," Vonlai said.

"Okay. Only one more bite, though."

As they walked through camp, swirls of dust slapped their faces. Vonlai shielded his mango, gnawing it till only the pit was left. Naked toddlers raced after one another, unaware of the gloom that surrounded them.

Something caught Vonlai's eye and he feared the mango would come right back up. "So it wasn't a ghost after all!"

"Ghost?" Dalah asked. "What are you talking about?"

Vonlai pointed.

It was the raspy-voiced shadow from the night before. Struggling to carry a bucket of water. Sloshing most of it over the side. Dragging the lame foot.

"That miserable soul would be better off dead," Dalah said.

Vonlai watched over his shoulder. Every step on the twisted, misshapen foot looked painful. "Is there no one to help?"

"Don't stare," Dalah said, pulling Vonlai along.

Old men with worn, sagging faces sat in a small group on the ground. One man scratched inside his ear with a stick and recounted how camp authorities had thrown out two former Pathet Lao soldiers. They had snuck into Na Pho seeking asylum alongside everyone else. Another man spit at the thought.

"*Oi!* They come here begging now that their stomachs are empty, too. Must be no more Lao gold to steal."

Flashes of a memory swamped Vonlai's mind. It must have been sometime shortly after the war ended in 1975, before Vonlai started first grade. Soldiers—in his house. Meh crying. Dalah crouched in a corner. The Pathet Lao had come for their gold. When they left, Meh cursed them out loud. Pah slapped his hand over her mouth. It was the bracelets she mourned the most. The 24-karat-gold birth bracelets Vonlai and Dalah had worn as babies. Family treasures lost forever.

Vonlai never told his parents he didn't care much about his bracelet. When the Communists took control of Laos, the most unsettling changes for him were his parents' new habit of whispering and their waning good humor. He didn't concern himself with such things as stolen baby jewelry. He loved soccer and swimming and slingshots, and above all else, Vonlai loved school.

But now, as the pulp of the fruit he'd swallowed drenched his gut with guilt, Vonlai wrestled with a sentiment his mind could not fully grasp. An infant's gold bracelet. A scavenger who rifled through their bags. And the mango he'd stolen. Was his character so thin that a few hours without food devoured his integrity? A thief, after all, is a thief, he'd always thought.

Vonlai shuddered as a sense of loss pecked at the

45

deepest part of him. He thought back to what he had learned or overheard from his parents about the Communist takeover so many years ago. Pah was an architect once, but after the war, there was no money to rebuild the structures destroyed by bombs. Even so, Pah was more fortunate than most because he had knowledge. Knowledge that was valuable to the Pathet Lao, who wanted the best properties for themselves. They knew Pah could tell them where to find them, so Pah had no choice but to lead them to the places that would most please them. The Pathet Lao paid homeowners a tiny bit of money, took the land and houses for themselves, then rewarded Pah with a can of gas, a bag of rice, or a bit of cash. And they didn't steal his scooter. Or kick him out of his house. Or make him disappear in the middle of the night.

But Pah and Meh never spoke of a prosperous future. There was no way to improve life. No way to have freedom of thought. And that was the loss that Vonlai's parents struggled with the most.

One of Vonlai's earliest memories was sharing a book with Pah that was filled with mesmerizing pictures. A fantasy world, Vonlai had thought, a magical place built with diamonds. After the Communists took over, the book had to be hidden away, but in Vonlai's eighth year his father pulled it from a nook in the ceiling. Pah told him it was a secret book for family only. Vonlai stared in wonder at the dazzling pictures of great American cities with sprawling skylines and towering buildings. Pah wanted Vonlai to know there was a world outside the oppression of Laos, where people spoke openly about ideas and didn't live in fear of their country's leaders.

Before the war ended, when Pah still had some work as an architect, he had designed houses for high-level Royal Lao officers who had important American military friends. A United States officer had given Vonlai's father the book—*Skyscrapers: Pillars of American Architecture*. Page after page showed mountains of steel and spotless glass reaching up in a paradise half a planet away. Vonlai was rapt when Pah told stories about skyscrapers disappearing into clouds.

One day, Vonlai and Khom, along with Khom's cousin, Souk, attached potato wheels to tin-can cars. They talked about what they would be when they grew up.

"An international soccer star, of course," Khom announced.

"A soldier," Souk said.

"I'll be an architect," said Vonlai, eyeballing the wheels and then testing the balance of the opposing vegetables.

"An archi-what?"

"A building builder," Vonlai answered. "I want to build skyscrapers, like in America. Their buildings are so tall, they touch the clouds."

"That's a lie!" Souk snapped.

Vonlai's head rattled with a lesson his father taught years ago: Be honorable and tell the truth. It was a lesson Pah stopped preaching once the Communists were in power, but it had taken root nevertheless.

"It's true," Vonlai insisted. "My father has a book. I've seen the pictures myself."

"My father says America is evil, and only white devils live there."

"Maybe so," Vonlai answered. "But those white devils know how to build buildings that touch the sky."

Vonlai sheltered a quiet pride at making his case.

Two days later, a knock at Vonlai's front door had rattled the windows.

"Take Vonlai and get to your room," Meh told Dalah. "Now."

Vonlai peeked out the window. Dalah tried to pull him down, but he shrugged her off.

Two Pathet Lao soldiers pulled Pah into the front yard. They were young—teenagers, Vonlai had thought, but they spoke sternly, poking their fingers into Pah's chest.

"You have a book that glorifies greedy American imperialists?"

"Those evil bastards—you must lust after their tramps, too!"

Vonlai's dog yipped at the soldiers' heels, her black fur

raised along her back, until she got a boot in the side and ran away howling.

Pah kept his eyes cast downward. The shorter soldier raised his hand to strike. Vonlai winced, but his father held his shoulders firm. The palm smacked Pah's cheek. They pushed him toward the house. Pah came through the door while the soldiers waited outside.

A minute later, Pah went back out carrying the secret book.

Vonlai shuddered as a thousand goose bumps rose up, mountains of fleshy guilt erupting on his skin.

The soldiers flipped through the pages without really looking and closed the book. They held it out for Vonlai's father, but as he reached for it, the shorter one pulled it away.

Both soldiers acted as if they'd heard the best joke, then slammed the book to the ground. The taller one, with black moles speckling his pockmarked face, dumped gasoline over it and set the book ablaze. "Don't ever forget," he said, his nose almost touching Pah's, "the party holds your life in its hands."

Vonlai licked his lips and swallowed the salty tears that spilled down his face.

Pah came inside to find Vonlai hiding under a bamboo chair. He lifted him off the floor and dried Vonlai's tears on his shirt.

"They can't burn what's in your mind, Vonlai. Your

mind and your dreams are your own, and you can't let them steal your hope."

From then on, his father stopped telling stories about America, but Vonlai repeated the old ones to himself and drew the pictures in his mind so he wouldn't forget. And Vonlai *did* dream, while vowing never to betray Pah's trust again. He dreamed of one day seeing those architectural marvels with his own eyes. Building a life for himself as strong as skyscrapers, double-decker bridges, underground trains, and soaring highways that looped up and around one another like ribbon on a gift.

Chapter
6

"This is it, Little Brother," Dalah said, pointing through an open doorway. "That's where you'll go to school."

"It doesn't look like a school. Where are the books?"

"There's a teacher, and there are students. That makes it a school."

The room was larger than their barracks—maybe twice the size, with a faded blackboard and one long bamboo table, but otherwise no different. Same dirt floor. Same sheet metal walls. Same hot, stagnant, stinking smell.

"Excuse me," a woman said, smiling. "Do you have your entry papers?"

"No, ma'am," Vonlai said. "My father is seeing about that."

"And I'm too old," Dalah said, her shoulders straight and seemingly proud.

The woman smiled. "I'm sure you'll be a big help to your brother, then."

Vonlai wanted to start right away. The woman's smile was so warm, it eased the worry that swelled inside him. But what about Dalah? There was nothing for her. The man at the processing center had said school stopped after sixth grade.

Dalah tugged on Vonlai's sleeve, her eyes an empty well. "Let's go home. You'll be back as soon as Pah gets the papers."

Home. What a strange word to be uttered in this place. *It didn't belong here*, Vonlai thought. There was too much sameness from barrack to barrack, worn face to worn face. Vonlai imagined himself back in Laos, rounding the banyan tree at breakneck speed on his way home from school. Home to his real house, where Meh managed to make their ransacked place beautiful by growing flowers the Pathet Lao saw no value in stealing. But here in Na Pho, there was no point in rushing home. There was even less here to eat. No chickens to feed. No market to explore. No Khom waiting with his soccer ball.

Vonlai's ears picked up bits of the teacher's lesson. Was that English she spoke? A shudder shot through him, colliding with his hunger, but it stirred his soul. He couldn't wait to come back to school. If he had to lose his home, he would hang on to his dreams. Pah taught him that.

"Dalah, what will you do all day while I'm at school?"

"Oh, there's plenty to be done. Meh will need help with the garden."

Excited shouts came from beyond building #27. "Run, run, run!"

A *thunk*—and cheers. "Goooal!"

Dalah and Vonlai rounded the building to a welcome sight.

A game of soccer was in play behind the latrines. Vonlai rushed to the sidelines, with Dalah two steps behind.

The sun beat down as the deep brown bodies—half shirts, half skins—pounded the ground. Bamboo poles formed makeshift goalposts. Every color of rubber sandal lined the edge of the field. They were useless for running. It was better to control the ball with bare feet.

Kids too young for school did rock patrol, hunting and hurling the intruders off to the side. Girls Dalah's age and older sat on the sidelines, chatting as they picked lice from one another's hair.

A boy, maybe twelve or thirteen, rushed close to Vonlai and flung himself on the ground, legs sprawled. "I'm whipped. Go in for me?"

"Me?" Vonlai looked at Dalah as if he'd been chosen for the highest honor.

"It's okay. Go," she said, pushing him. "Hurry."

Vonlai flicked off his flip-flops, tore off his shirt, and

ran in. He raced toward the goal, chasing the ball carrier, who was two heads taller than him and bald as a monk. He caught up in no time and stole the ball away.

"Here, Skeleton Boy," someone called from downfield. "Pass it!"

Vonlai flicked it easily across the field and ran down the sideline. And the boys wasted no time giving him valiant chase. On the field, they weren't refugees, ill-fed and filthy. They were soccer stars, delivering glory to their homeland and honor to their families.

"Vonlai!" a voice called.

Had he already made fans? Khom used to play like that back in Laos. Running one on one against Vonlai, Khom would chant his own name, dreaming of the day when a packed stadium came to cheer him on at the World Cup. Vonlai sank into his fantasy and raised his arms in mock acceptance of the fanfare.

"Vonlai! Vonlai!"

He turned to the chanter, ready to take a bow. He felt his face flush when he saw that his adoring fan was really his annoyed mother. Meh stood with her hands on her hips, Dalah by her side. Vonlai ran off the field.

"You worried me, boy," Meh said. "You've been gone nearly half the day."

"Sorry, Meh, but can you believe there's soccer here?"

"You'll be in school soon, anyway. And I told you

not to leave Dalah."

"He didn't leave me, Meh. I was right there on the sidelines. I met a girl my age."

"Well, Pah's not happy you've been away so long. This place is no playground. There are desperate people here. Desperate people do desperate things."

"We didn't need the reminder," Dalah said. "We're part of those desperate people."

"I'm reminding you to watch out for each other. I forbid you to be alone, Dalah."

Meh stormed off the field with Dalah. Vonlai trailed after them.

The tall teen who squared up against Vonlai ran over and held out his hand. "Nice play, Skeleton Boy. Coming back tomorrow?"

"Maybe. If I don't start school yet."

"School? How old are you?" He shook his bald head and sweat flew everywhere.

"Twelve. I'm in sixth grade."

"Why bother? It's only a few more months, anyway. You want to waste those lightning legs sitting around running numbers through your head—then what? Gives me a headache just thinking about it."

"I think you have a headache 'cause your hair's trying to grow."

"Very funny, skinny man. Just wait till the nits take

over your head. You'll be bald, too."

"I have to go," Vonlai said, turning his shirt right side out. "I'll see you around. What's your name?"

"Kavin."

"Thanks, Kavin. You better get back in there. Your team's getting walloped."

Vonlai jogged to catch up to Meh and Dalah, but a stomach cramp nearly knocked him down. His body had used up every last bit of energy and it demanded food. In two days he'd eaten only the palmful of rice and half a mango. He rested his hands on his knees to stay upright. Kavin's question about the end of school rang in his head. *Then what?*

Vonlai didn't want to think about "then." Pah had said they would get in and out of Na Pho quickly. Vonlai didn't expect to be in the refugee camp after he'd finished sixth grade. Surely they'd have a new home by then. A new country. But Kavin didn't seem to have any hope of leaving soon. He had settled on soccer as the focus of camp life and spoke as if it were obvious Vonlai would still be here when he finished school.

Vonlai felt eyes bore into him. He saw the limping figure sitting on the ground hunched over his lap. A man, probably, based on the short sarong he had tucked around his middle and between his legs. His head tilted sideways to fix his gaze on Vonlai. He ran his finger over something cupped in his hand. Vonlai couldn't make it out, but he saw that the man treated it with care. He stroked it as if it were a pet mouse. Then Vonlai saw a glint of light. A knife clutched in the man's hand, its blade bouncing the sun into Vonlai's eyes.

Vonlai imagined the man severing the head of some poor captured creature and swallowing the thing whole.

Desperate people do desperate things.

Vonlai straightened as much as he could and headed after his family. The man grunted and waved the knife at him, gesturing toward something—but what? Vonlai stopped cold. Was it a threat? A warning? A crazed display?

Vonlai kept walking, trying to make sense of what the man wanted him to see. He stubbed his bare toe on a pile of rocks the kids had stacked, and remembered—his sandals. Vonlai ran back to fetch them, but they were gone. Surely a thief wouldn't have chosen his ratty pair above all others to steal, but he was certain he'd left them by the fence post. Vonlai imagined Pah shaking his head in disappointment when he'd have to admit losing his only pair of shoes.

Vonlai had to search more—maybe the hunger distorted his memory of where he'd kicked them off. He turned back and walked up the field's boundary, his eyes scouring the ground. After several steps, he nearly bumped into the old man. His knife was outstretched,

Vonlai's flip-flops dangling off the blade. Vonlai choked on his own sudden breath.

"The meat trucks come Wednesday," the man said in a voice that sounded like he had a throat full of thistles.

Vonlai swallowed hard, took his shoes, and nodded slowly to show his thanks.

Meat. On Wednesday. He had five more days to wait, but the man had given him something to look forward to. And that was enough for now.

Chapter
7

Pah folded a stack of documents and carefully packed them in a tattered bag. "You begin school on Monday, son."

Every pore on Vonlai's body tingled. After all that'd happened over the past month—the Mekong crossing, the miserable weeks in Nong Khai, and the long bus trip to Na Pho—Vonlai wanted to shout his joy. But he merely nodded at Pah's announcement. He had seen Dalah's face fall, souring the good news. Her expression mirrored the look of those sitting in the dust when they entered camp, withered and worn.

Vonlai changed the subject. "Can we wash tonight?"

"If you fill all the jugs," Meh said, pouring freshly boiled drinking water into old liquor bottles. "Better hurry. The water station closes at six."

"Come on, Dalah," Vonlai said. "I think there's a breeze tonight."

"Since when do you volunteer to clean yourself up?" Dalah joked, pinching her nose.

"Since there's no river to do it for me."

Vonlai and Dalah grabbed all the containers they could carry and dumped them into the wheelbarrow—plastic vinegar buckets and rectangular cans that once held cooking oil. Their tops had been sheared off and bamboo sticks driven through the sides to serve as handles.

As they made their way to the water station, Dalah and Vonlai saw Thai villagers set up shop on their carts outside the refugee camp gates. They sold small goods to camp volunteers and staff, and to any refugee who had a bit of cash.

A man on a bicycle rode past, a pack of underwear clutched under his arm and a bundle of cilantro in his teeth. He cut in front of Vonlai, kicking his feet out like a boy on a brand-new bike, and zigzagged through camp.

"Where'd he get *that*?" Vonlai asked.

"Guess he bought it," Dalah said. "Must know he's going to be here awhile to blow money on a bike."

"Maybe Meh would buy me—"

"Don't you dare ask," Dalah said. "She'll skin you on the spot, and then I'll be all alone."

Vonlai watched as the man rode through camp like royalty, refugees parting to make way. His tires left tracks in the dirt like a viper escaping into the scrub.

Vonlai imagined how it would feel to ride his own

bicycle again. He remembered leaning it against the house the day they left Laos. His wheel had gotten twisted, and Pah said he'd straighten it the next day. Vonlai knew Pah'd make it good as new, but by morning, they were gone.

Even though that rusty heap was more fit for an eight-year-old, Vonlai knew that under the Pathet Lao, he was lucky to have it. He and Khom sometimes worked up the nerve to beg a kip off their mothers. Khom would ride the handlebars while Vonlai pedaled into market, a two-man parade. They pooled their money and haggled with vendors for the biggest piece of chicken on a stick. And Vonlai knew of a newspaper vendor who secretly sold western magazines. He longed for a peek at western architecture so he'd have something more progressive than his village to draft in the dirt. And Khom was always up for a bit of mischief. They waited till the vendor busied himself, then sneaked to his cart while he made change for a customer.

"Now!" Vonlai whispered, pushing Khom's back.

Khom lifted a stack of newspapers and snatched a magazine from underneath. He passed it to Vonlai, who scurried behind a heap of boxes. Vonlai would take a quick look, then return it. He'd never bring shame to his family by sinking to thievery.

His fingers trembled. He opened it slowly to minimize the creaking of fresh pages.

Vonlai and Khom hunched over the magazine,

thumbing past articles to find pictures of American cities. "Ouch!" Vonlai yelled.

The vendor thumped Vonlai's head and snatched the magazine back. He leaned in close so no one else could hear and spewed a garlic-filled rage. "Stupid boys—holding it in the open for all to see! *Oi!* You've greased up the pages with your filthy dog paws."

He rolled up the magazine and whacked Vonlai on the head. *Bap! Bap! Bap!*

Khom laughed, and the vendor turned to swing at him. He pretzeled his way out of the first whack and dodged more blows until Vonlai could grab his bike. Khom ran alongside him, his legs pumping as if he had a clear shot at an open goal.

The vendor shook his balled fist after them. "I'll tell the soldiers you stole from my cart! They'll drag your families off to seminar camp and work you till you die!"

At the water station, Vonlai held his old oil can under the spigot and wondered about those families who *did* go to seminar camp.

In Laos, he'd make himself appear preoccupied so he could eavesdrop on hushed adult conversations. He'd heard how men were taken to seminar camps after the Communists won the war. Flown in Soviet choppers, maybe to an old Pathet Lao camp on the Plain of Jars, or maybe hidden places in the northern mountains around Viengxay. What was promised to be only a few months of "educational seminars" turned into years of brutal indoctrination, and the men never returned. Wives and children sometimes went to visit and didn't return, either. And whispers swirled that even King Sisavang Vatthana, Queen Khamboui, and Say Vongsavang, the crown prince of Laos, were forced to go. Under the Communist government, everyone had to be reeducated—brainwashed into the new way of thinking. Forced into hard labor, carrying on their backs the wood they'd cut to build shelter. Working the earth to grow vegetables if they wanted to eat. Nobody knew where the royal family was imprisoned—or if they were still alive.

"Hey, your bucket's full." Vonlai felt a flick of water hit his ear. Dalah stood waiting as she slid a finger under the scarf that hid her hair. "I'm about to shave off this rat's nest if I can't get it washed."

Dalah's new friend, Jun, ran over, her dirty sarong dragging on the ground. "Hey, you want to come hang out? My friend has a guitar."

"We can't," Vonlai said. "We're due back home."

"She was talking to me," said Dalah.

"It's no big deal," Jun said, picking up a bucket to help load the wheelbarrow. "He can come."

"No." Dalah grabbed the bucket from Jun. Water sloshed out, turning the dirt at Dalah's feet black. "Meh wants to get water boiling. We have nothing to drink."

"But Meh boiled the drinking—"

"Little Brother, I'm talking!" Dalah jerked Vonlai's elbow, pulling him close to bark in his ear. "You'll make friends at school. You don't need to steal mine!"

Jun scooped up her skirt as she trotted backward. "Well, we'll be on the ridge behind the temple." She ran off to join a boy waiting in the shade of a building. "Come later if you want."

The boy waved a long arm at Vonlai. It was the bald player from the soccer field.

"Who's that?" Dalah asked.

"Kavin. I played soccer with him."

Dalah watched him head up the hill with Jun and a few others. "He's tall." She loaded her last bucket and left.

"Hey, I'm not done yet," Vonlai called. "We're supposed to stay together."

"So hurry it up. And don't whine like a baby."

In front of the barracks, Pah was shoring up the chest-high shower screen that was attached to the outside of their room. He braced the side with a tree limb and used a knife handle to hammer loose nails.

Meh squatted by a tree stump and used the top for a cutting board. She chopped a stalk of bok choy.

"We have vegetables?" Vonlai asked. A flutter shot through him.

"From our neighbors," Meh said.

Vonlai pulled the lid off the pot. He let the steam flood his face. A drumstick bone floated in the starchy water. "Is that meat, too?"

"Just bone," Meh said. "They have young ones next door and were generous to share what they could. Now close that lid unless you want to eat raw rice."

Vonlai saw Dalah perk up at the thought of bone marrow to flavor the meal. She untied the scarf from her head and held it between pinched fingertips. "This thing's dripping with grease. Want me to toss it under the pot to give the fire a boost?"

"Now that's teamwork," Pah said.

Sitting on a mat in front of their barracks, Vonlai's family shared a meal. Refugees called out to one another from across the way. "Got anything good to eat there, neighbor?"

Their rice was watery and stale, and the chicken bone did more to feed their imaginations than it did to season the rice.

"Of course! We've butchered a cow, and the sticky rice is sweet," Pah hollered.

"Oo-ee." Meh clicked her tongue, savoring a delicious thought. "I made nam jeel so spicy, you'd swear you were eating fire."

"And to top it off," Vonlai called, "we have coconut

milk and potatoes for dessert."

He tipped his bowl to drink up the last of his rice. His stomach ached a little less, and just like the prisoners trying to survive Communist labor camps, Vonlai had embraced a new mind-set that might keep him from dying.

Chapter
8

Sunday afternoon came and Vonlai was restless. All morning long, Dalah had lingered around the barracks, and Vonlai didn't want to go off by himself.

Dalah's cycle had come. Meh ripped a towel and folded the strips for her to bleed on. There was only enough for one day, so the cloths had to be rinsed and hung to dry in plain view. It was enough to keep Dalah stifled in the room, with no breeze to stir the stagnant air.

Vonlai wished away the day so he could start school. The buzz in his bones made him fidget.

"Keep away from me," Dalah said.

"Where am I supposed to go?"

"I don't care. Just away."

"Everyone has their stuff hanging outside," Vonlai said, scratching away the scab where a mosquito had feasted. "My underwear is out there, too."

"Ugh! Are you playing father now? I don't need a lecture. Just be glad you're not a girl."

Vonlai nudged a lizard that was perched in the corner behind the bed. It skittered and zagged its way out the door, stalling for a second in the streak of sunlight.

Dalah sat up, cradling her abdomen and rocking on the edge of the bed. "I hate this place."

"I know," Vonlai answered. "I hate it, too, but we won't be here forever."

"How do you know? Jun's been here since she was ten. That's almost four years, Little Brother. Four years! She doesn't even talk about getting out anymore."

Dalah got up to pace around the room. She grabbed a knife and edged around her fingernails to clean out the dirt. "Countries are starting to deny refugees now. I've heard people say it. Nobody wants us. They don't think about the war anymore, or people like us with no place to live."

"But doesn't Dad have a cousin in America? That's supposed to help, right?"

"Don't you know anything? Dad was just a civilian. The military families get priority."

Vonlai tossed a rubber ball against the wall. Each throw got harder and harder, the hollow smacks damming his ears. The last throw rebounded off the wall and zipped back over his head. It bounced into a corner, bobbling itself to silence.

"Come with me to the soccer field," he said. "If you don't get out of here today, you'll be stuck in here all week while I'm at school."

"Lucky you." She tossed the knife in a cooking pot, black from layers of smoke and oil. "Leave me alone then for a minute, so I can clean myself."

Vonlai sat on the tree stump waiting. He heard the sloshing of water inside the room, and the graduated *drip, drip, drip,* of a cloth getting wrung. He scratched his name in the dirt with a chopstick.

Vonlai Sirivong was here.

Dalah ran past, flicking his ear.

"Hey, grease face!" Vonlai jumped up, his foot smearing the marks. "You can't go without me!"

Vonlai gave chase, ducking under clothes and towels and bedding draped between barracks. A white strap caught his shoulder. He stopped to pull it off, but the other end boinged off the line, wrapping his face. He wrangled with it, elbows flailing—a cricket caught in spider silk.

"You urchin!" a woman screamed. She railed one hand against Vonlai's ear and snatched back her bra with the other. "For shame—stealing ladies' underthings! I'll tell the guards there's a pervert on the loose!"

"Ah-ha-ha!" Kavin called from his shower screen across the way, bubbles dripping down his bald head.

"Skeleton Boy likes girlie things!"

"Sorry, Aunt. So sorry!" Vonlai told the woman as he backed away, his hands held together in a show of respect.

He ran to catch Dalah.

"You going to the field?" Kavin yelled after him.

"Yeah, come on!" Vonlai rounded a block of toilets and nearly smacked into Dalah, her back pinned against the latrine wall, eyes downcast. A guard held her shoulders. It was the same guard who had tossed the cigarette on Vonlai's foot.

"Hey, little man," the guard said, a sneer warping his face. "I told your sister here to slow down." He dropped his hands off her shoulders. "Wouldn't want anyone getting hurt. Why, there's barely enough medical care to help the dying, much less a careless girl. Or do you fancy yourself a woman yet?"

"She's fourteen," Vonlai said.

"No, I'm not. I turned fifteen the third week in Nong Khai."

Vonlai tried to understand how time could pass unnoticed.

"Well, most certainly a woman, then," the guard said, smoothing a mustache barely the size of a rice noodle, and looking at Dalah too long.

"Can we go now?" Vonlai asked.

"Of course," the guard said, adjusting his belt as he

walked away. "Remember: Don't be careless."

Dalah closed her eyes and released a ragged breath. "What took you so long?" she asked, her jaw tight, her voice unsteady.

"I was right behind you."

She straightened her sarong and started up the hill. "Yeah, I guess you were. Maybe I can outrun you one of these days."

"Doubt it," Vonlai said. "I'd have to let you win."

Dalah punched his arm. "You better not, dog-face!"

"Well, hurry then."

Kavin rushed up behind Vonlai and leapfrogged over his shoulders. "Hey, man. I want you on *my* team this time."

"What makes you think I want *you*, Grandpa?"

"Easy now. Respect your elders," Kavin said, but his eyes were on Dalah. "What's your name, anyway, Skeleton Boy?"

"Vonlai."

"And who's this?" Kavin asked. "Your sister?"

"My name is Dalah. Vonlai's *older* sister."

"You going to watch us play, Older Sister Dalah?" Kavin bounced a little, practicing his footwork and kicking imaginary soccer balls.

"Yeah, I guess," Dalah said. "There's not a whole lot else to do." She noticed Jun already sitting along the sidelines with a deck of cards and ran to grab a spot. She whispered in Jun's ear. They both turned to look at Kavin, a smile swelling on Dalah's face.

Vonlai stood at the field's edge, waiting for someone to tap his shoulder so he could go in.

Behind the goal, Vonlai saw him, under a tree. The old man, hunched over his lap again, a tiny pile of wood stacked beside him. The man's knife flew over a chunk, shavings and flecks collecting on his legs.

"What's that guy doing over there?" Vonlai asked.

Kavin looked briefly, then turned his eyes back to the game. "Same thing we are, Little Brother. Just passing the time."

Vonlai watched the old man hold out the piece of wood and examine it from all angles. He ran his finger along one side over and over, rubbing as if the wood were clay. Something in the shape must have dissatisfied him—he chucked the whole thing over his shoulder. The old man scooped up the other pieces from the pile at his side and studied each of them before choosing one to carve. The knife seemed like an extension of the man's bony fingers, but straight and clean, not riddled with knots.

The guys on the field cheered as the ball shot past the goal, smacking the side of a latrine. A woman inside screamed and cursed and vowed revenge, calling on ancestors to punish the rotten lot. The field erupted in laughter, but Vonlai couldn't take his eyes off the old man. He saw what he was doing—taking a shapeless piece of nothing and turning it into something beautiful.

Chapter
9

Vonlai barely slept the night before school started. Snores rattled the stillness around him. The song of crickets ebbed and swelled against the occasional yips of dogs fighting in the distance.

He crawled over Meh, careful not to snag her hair under his knees. He slipped past the mosquito net and out of bed. Pah had rigged their door shut with wire and nails. Vonlai untwisted it and sat outside on the mat to watch the sky. It was endless and thick and full of wonder. Vonlai could sit there all night holding on to the anticipation of what might lie ahead. He didn't want morning to arrive. He didn't want another reality to spoil the vision that soothed his soul.

A shooting star fell across the horizon. *Where does such a thing begin?* Vonlai wondered. It comes from nowhere to soar gloriously across the sky—for just an instant—and disappears forever. Was he the only one to see it? What if he hadn't come outside? What's the point of such a beautiful flight if it ends without crossing the path of someone who can appreciate it?

Vonlai fell asleep against the wall, his mind sated with an imaginary trail of shooting stars, lasting long enough so everyone could see it and soak up its light.

Pah tapped Vonlai's shoulder. "Boy, are you sick?"

"Is it time?" Vonlai rubbed his neck to work out a kink.

"If you're well, I'll walk you to the school."

Vonlai was up in a second. He splashed water on his face and went inside to pull on a shirt. Meh rolled up a Ping-Pong-ball-size of rice, sprinkled it with a trace of salt, and handed it to him for breakfast, along with a wet cloth.

"Clean your neck, too, and inside your ears."

Dalah was still in bed, curled into herself despite the heat.

Pah walked with him on his way to the processing building.

"Where are you going, Pah?"

"There are new refugees coming every week. Many cannot read or write. I've offered my services to the Joint Volunteer Agency while we're here, to help fill out their documents."

"The JVA?" Vonlai asked. "Do you get a name tag like Keng, that man who brought our rice?"

Pah reached in his pocket and produced the green name tag with English letters.

"Ah—let me see it!" Vonlai said. He snatched it from Pah and studied the letters of his father's name as he walked alongside him. *B-O-U-N-E.*

At the doorway to school, Pah held out his hand. "I need that back. Now go learn how to spell your own name. And help Meh and your sister when you're out of school. I'll be back this evening."

Vonlai looked for someone familiar to sit by. He stifled a growing fear as he realized most of the kids in school were younger than him. Had all the other twelve-year-olds given up, not wanting to waste their bit of energy baking in a box filled with little kids?

The teacher invited him to find a spot. "Welcome, Vonlai. I am Miss Chada."

Miss Chada looked fresh and clean. Her eyes shone bright, and her black hair, twisted on top of her head, captured bits of light. Her smile comforted Vonlai. "Thank you, ma'am. Are you the teacher for all the kids here?" he asked.

"Yes. Come in, please."

"You mean you teach the little ones, too? In the same class?"

"There are common lessons to be learned no matter what the age."

Miss Chada began a lesson in English. It sounded like a snake. *Ts-ss-sss, puh-tss-sh-sss.* Vonlai looked at a boy sitting across from him. He was pale and barely mouthing the words. Vonlai wished he had a tissue to give the boy so he could wipe his nose and dab the gray mucus clogging the corners of his eyes.

Vonlai turned his attention to Miss Chada. He had to focus. This is what he'd been waiting for. Ever since the day he dragged himself out of the Mekong and onto the banks of Thailand, Vonlai had built his dreams on the opportunities that school could bring.

He concentrated on Miss Chada's lips as they formed the English words, strange and hissing. He prayed if he could somehow pick up the language right away, be at the top of his class, fill his mind with lessons so the knowledge could spill over to feed his spirit, that he might be able to earn himself a quicker escape from this place.

Being wrong was not a concept he wanted to consider.

Chapter
10

Children ran squealing past Vonlai's doorway. The trucks had come. It was Wednesday. Finally Wednesday, and the meat trucks had come. Three of them—a cloud of dust framing their arrival against a smoldering sunset. Older refugees lingered outside, their eyes slightly wider than the day before, waiting for their portion.

Vonlai fought the urge to sprint. "Are we supposed to go up there? How do they know we're here?"

"Our paperwork has been filed," Meh said. "They know we're here."

"How much do we get? Is it chicken? Fish? What?"

"Vonlai, your impatience will change nothing," Meh said, scraping a layer of soot-coated grease off her rice pot. But her shoulders seemed straighter. Vonlai could see her face, softer, more relaxed. Pah napped on a mat laid out close to the building in a strip of shade.

"There is a representative assigned to collect the portion for our building," Pah said. He didn't open his eyes. "He'll split it among us. I've been assured we'll get what's due."

"Well, I'm going to see."

"Me too," Dalah said, sliding her feet into her slippers.

Men pushing wobbly carts made their way to the trucks. The crowd stepped back, allowing them to position themselves up front. Each building representative handed a slip of paper to the men squatting on the truck beds.

A toddler brushed against Vonlai's leg. His naked body was streaked with grime, one eye nearly swollen shut from mosquito bites.

"Hey, buddy," Vonlai said, looking around for a parent or sibling to come fetch him. The boy looked up and held his arms out to Vonlai.

"Whose kid is that?" Dalah asked, squatting down to peek into his face.

"No idea," Vonlai said.

"Well, he likes you. Pick him up before he gets trampled."

Vonlai lifted the boy over his head and parked him on his shoulders. The boy shrieked and clapped, kicking his bare feet against Vonlai's chest.

"I know how you feel, little man," Vonlai said, hooking his arms around the boy's feet.

The crowd was buoyant but guarded. Vonlai wanted to

remember their expressions, capture their eagerness. Hope showed in their eyes, lighting up each dusty face like a fresh green leaf landing on a monsoon puddle.

How long had these people been here? How long would they stay? There were women, their middles bulging, ready to introduce new faces into this place. Strong men who'd recently arrived, with tattooed arms that still rippled with muscles not yet withered. The thief who rifled through their things was surely among the crowd, too. And the old man hovering in back, supporting himself against a fence post.

Vonlai searched for the person who might represent his building. Was he someone who had shown him kindness? A fair man who could be trusted to parcel out the correct portions? Or was he a shifty con, elbowing his way into this coveted position?

"Sure is a ton of food on those trucks," Vonlai said.

"Yeah," Dalah said, tickling the toddler's foot. "For a thousand people, maybe. But there's three times that in Na Pho."

Camp staff and refugees who were assigned to the task unloaded box after box to the men waiting below.

A body slammed into Dalah and ricocheted to the ground. She opened her mouth to protest, but Vonlai pulled her back. He'd seen a Thai guard smack the teenaged boy.

"Settle down, you Lao white-eyed chicken!" the guard

roared. "You couldn't even defend your own country—now you come begging your way into Thailand kicking up dust. Stay back!"

When the guard turned away to hassle his next target, Vonlai reached out to help the boy, still balancing the toddler on his shoulders. "You okay?" he asked.

The teen stood up, and Dalah brushed gravel off his back.

"Is *anybody* okay in this place?" he answered, his wide eyes darting. He sneaked around the opposite side of the truck bed, reaching between its rails for something to steal. He got a slap on the head instead, this time from the guard who'd cornered Dalah.

The men finished unloading the boxes. The representatives pushed their carts toward the barracks, their dedicated flock following close behind.

A woman scurried to Vonlai, dragging a girl no more than four by the hand. She pulled the boy from his shoulders. "*Oi*, you orphan!" she said, snuggling the boy's neck. "Come on home, Noy. They won't have any more to eat at their house."

Every rice pot was on to boil. The soccer field was deserted. Hundreds of smoke plumes twirled skyward, decorating the landscape like a sea of dancing kite tails.

"Over here, Savat," a man called. The group had gathered in front of a barracks halfway down Vonlai's building.

The man held out his tin pan. "Me first, please. My wife may have that baby before she's had a chance at a decent meal."

"This week again?" Savat called, splitting open a box top. "We've heard that story three weeks running now. How about something new, Pasong?"

Savat grabbed a frozen chicken by the head, tossed it on a scale, then split another bird down the middle to add to it. Savat nodded, and his wife tossed the mangled carcasses, three small papayas, and a head of cabbage into the man's tray. "Off you go," the wife said. "There'll be nothing left to beg when we're through."

Meh stood in line, a plastic tub at her side. Dalah and Vonlai joined her.

"Did you see that, Meh?" Vonlai whispered. "Just one skinny bird and half of another? Is that all we get, for a whole week?"

"You won't be complaining when it's sitting in your belly tonight."

"It's not tonight I'm worried about. It's the rest of the week."

Vonlai watched the boxes empty as people held out trays and banana leaves to collect their cut.

"Our turn," Dalah said, nudging Meh.

Savat threw a bird into her tub. Its feet flipped sideways now under the thawing heat.

"You're new," Savat's wife said to Meh, dropping in one large papaya and bok choy. "Take this fish sauce. It's nearly empty, but the staples truck won't come for two weeks yet. You may get a few days' worth of flavor from it."

"Your kindness doesn't go unnoticed," Meh said. She stayed in line waiting for more chicken.

"Sorry, Aunt," Savat said. "There are only four in your family. You have your share."

"Many thanks," Meh said, sidestepping the last five people.

"Meh," Dalah said through clenched teeth. "There's at least a dozen birds left in that box. That's almost three apiece for the others!"

"They aren't for the others, Dalah." Meh balanced her tub on her hip as she walked.

"That's stealing!" Vonlai said. "How can they get away with it?"

"I'm not so sure I wouldn't do the same," Meh said, quickening her pace. "Complaining children wear a woman down faster than hauling bricks up a mountain."

Vonlai turned to see the old man hold out a banana leaf to collect his share. It didn't appear the man had any family to care for. How much could his portion have been? Probably just a drumstick, Vonlai thought. What a bland soup that would make.

On their front stoop, Meh chopped off the chicken feet and tossed them into the pot first. Then she plucked the remaining feathers. She reached inside where the chicken was gutted. "Oh good, Father," she told Pah. "This is a lucky bird. Still has her liver and a sack of eggs."

Pah smiled. "Lucky indeed. We'll share those and let Dalah and Vonlai have a whole foot to themselves."

Meh did everything she could to make the meat last at least through Friday. She boiled it over the open flame to make a broth. She scraped off every bit of meat to flavor the rice. She broke the bones open to make it easier to suck out the marrow. And she boiled the shards all over again in the next pot of rice, dribbling a few extra drops of fish sauce into the pot.

Vonlai accepted what she gave him and never uttered one complaint.

Four days with nothing to eat but rice and limp vegetables was better than five.

Chapter
11

June 1982

The monsoon rains had turned the camp into a mud pit, the barrage of water pounding the metal roof like AK-47s. Vonlai sat in the doorway, a curtain of water spilling off the overhang. A russet river coursed between buildings, shifting filth from one end of camp to the other.

Nearly three months had passed since they left Laos. Vonlai had thought he'd turn thirteen in a new country, but here he sat in Na Pho, a teenager now, trying to forget the passing time. He had settled into a routine of school, soccer, and averting his hunger. The monotony of Dalah's days, in which she sat with Meh in women's circles after cleaning and cooking chores were done, made her eager to go exploring when Vonlai returned from school. They discovered remote corners with the best breeze and smallest view of crimped roofs that wrapped lopsided buildings. In the heat of late afternoons, before dinner fires were lit, they could drift off to sleep there, escaping into a world where the wind carried their minds to anyplace but Na Pho.

Vonlai had learned quickly to skip any breakfast Meh could scrounge up and save his portion for dinner. A morning meal only awakened his hunger that much earlier, and an empty stomach at the day's start was better than at bedtime. At least during daylight, he could sit through a few hours in school and keep his brain busy—Miss Chada praised him for being so studious, so attentive.

But at night, on an empty stomach, Vonlai's mind fell easily to nightmares. Images of his family hanging dead from trees. Pathet Lao soldiers laughing, watching him sink in a ratty boat in the middle of the Mekong River, Khom's bloated corpse floating by.

Once the rains stopped, the steam bath started. The humid air roused the days-old sweat on Vonlai's body. "I'm washing now," he told Meh.

"We're low on water. Can't you wait till the station opens?"

"I can smell my own stink," Vonlai said, waving away his stench. "I don't want to walk around all day reeking like an armpit."

"You should have washed last night when you had a chance to fill up the tank."

"I did wash—my feet, at least."

"Oh, really," Dalah called from inside the room, still in bed. "Then why am I lying on your crusty crumbs of dirt?"

"See, Meh? I need to wash."

"Make sure there's enough drinking water and save some for cooking," Meh said. "You'll have to fill up the tank this afternoon. Sounds like you and Dalah need to scrub the bedding today, anyway."

Every day required such an effort for basic tasks. Hauling water. Chopping wood. Scrubbing clothes. Always hungry. Always dirty. And the mosquitoes. Always mosquitoes, even after the trucks came, spraying their killer fog over camp, over larvae-infested puddles, over open rice pots.

The priority never wavered. Cooking rice was the most basic of needs, the driving force that made the weary wake up. Any water left over was used for washing. But too many times the day's supply was used up in the garden or to fill an aching gut, and the water station was turned off before laundry or bathing could be done.

Vonlai dipped from the water tank that sat behind the shower screen and filled their cooking pot halfway. He tried to fit on the lid, but it was bent, leaving a gap around the edge, so the water was slow to boil.

"Add another cupful," Meh said.

The rice trucks had come the day before, six of them, delivering the monthly rations. Meh always cooked an extra cup or so the day after the new rice came, good for teasing the stomach with a couple extra bites.

"Will we ever get anything but this steamed rice?" Vonlai asked. "It's more mildew and rocks than it is rice. Why can't they give us sticky rice once in a while?"

"Your stomach doesn't care what kind of rice it gets," Meh said, her gaze fixed on the steam seeping out from the crooked lid. "It's only your tongue that tastes the difference."

Vonlai craved traditional sticky rice. Its slightly sweet flavor and hearty texture was perfect for scooping up meat and pepper sauce. Even in sleep, he dreamed about it. Giant spreads, heaps of spicy papaya, fish and lime soup. And sticky rice. Steaming, fresh sticky rice. But Vonlai always awoke just before he could stuff a chunk in his mouth.

Pah used to say a meal without sticky rice is like an itch you can't scratch—it won't kill you, but it might drive you crazy.

Maybe Meh was right, Vonlai thought. *Would it really matter if they could have sticky rice for a change?* It would only remind him of home, and memories were dangerous, haunting. There were already crazy people running through Na Pho, caught between an ugly past and an uncertain future.

Vonlai and Dalah headed to the soccer fields. As usual, the old man was there, his back against a barren mango tree, his knife working the wood.

How long had that crippled soul been in this camp? Did he still look forward to the day when he would be free of this place, or had he given up like too many others?

Most refugees searched the list posted outside the processing center every week. The United Nations had found a place in the outside world willing to take some of them in, and the list showed the names of those next in line for exit interviews. Vonlai's hope waned every week his family name, Sirivong, did not appear in the *S* column. He checked every page, anyway, praying for a mistake.

But Vonlai never saw the old man looking there. He seemed indifferent, like he was right where he was supposed to be. He went about his business, never speaking out and never drawing attention to himself. The youngest children feared him, arching away from him when their paths were about to cross. Older kids ignored him altogether, passing by as if he were invisible. He was a living ghost. Why did he surround himself with kids when none of them paid him any attention?

Kavin sat on the sidelines and spread his shirt on the ground for Dalah to sit on.

"You're not playing today, Grandpa?" Vonlai asked. He thought Kavin was sitting way too close to Dalah to be comfortable in the heat.

"Taking a break for now," Kavin said. "Besides, you

show me up nearly every time. I'll watch you embarrass someone else for a bit." Kayin plucked pebbles from the ground as Dalah started telling a story, their heads leaning in close like bees sharing nectar.

Midway through the game, Vonlai took a break, but he left his sister and friend alone a while longer. He was glad Dalah would have Kavin's company while he was in school.

The old man was still carving. Vonlai stood in front of him as the man's foot jutted out at an awkward angle, twisted and knobby.

"What are you making?" Vonlai finally asked.

"Have you lost your manners, boy?"

"I'm sorry, Uncle," Vonlai said.

"You may call me Colonel."

Vonlai wondered about the man's rich imagination, to call himself Colonel. Any stretch of the mind to help the days pass, he supposed. Vonlai dropped to his knees so as not to hover over an elder. "May I see what you're making, please, Colonel?"

The man held up a tiny elephant and blew one last wood shaving from behind the ear. "It's a guardian for travelers. Take it. I can do no more with it."

"I don't think I'm traveling anywhere."

The man continued to hold out the elephant. "Doubt already seeped into your mind, eh? Better be careful. Your brain will rot and turn into a puddle swarming with parasites."

"Do you think you're getting out?" Vonlai asked, accepting the gift.

"I'm not fool enough to question my fate."

Vonlai helped pull the man up from the ground. He was shocked by how light he felt. His baggy clothes concealed a bony frame. Vonlai held out his arm for the man to lean on as they slowly walked, but the man sent Vonlai home. "You'll be late for dinner. Go to your family."

Vonlai almost responded, What dinner? But he was embarrassed at the idea of complaining to someone who seemed to be struggling to breathe. "The elephant is perfect," Vonlai said. "Thank you."

The man hobbled down the hill, his lopsided gait nearly toppling him.

Vonlai joined Dalah and her friend, Jun, on the sidelines. Kavin had gone in, charged the ball carrier, stole possession, and was off.

The guard with the wimpy mustache stood near and whistled for his turn to go in. Then he locked his eyes on Jun.

From midfield, Kavin raised his arm without hesitation to opt out. The guard's impatience had proven to be dangerous, his palm readily slapping away any ingrate who toyed with him. Kavin ran off field and stood next to

Dalah, blocking the guard's view of her.

"That guard's crazy," Jun said after he took his place on the field.

"Keep your mouth shut around him," Kavin warned.

"Who is he?" Dalah asked. She pulled her long ponytail around her shoulders and smoothed it down, a nervous habit Vonlai hadn't seen since they first arrived in Na Pho.

"Calls himself Tiger," Kavin said, and he beat his chest with a fist to imitate the guard. "Tiger Tong, I am. I'll swallow you whole."

Dalah pulled Jun's arm. "Come on, let's get out of here."

Dalah turned to give Kavin a soft smile. Vonlai saw her face, gentle and inviting, a face without one hint of the sly grin he was accustomed to. She looked like Meh. And Kavin stood dumbstruck as he watched Dalah walk away, ignoring the game behind him.

"Hey!" Vonlai hollered after the girls. "Hey! Where are you going?" He ran to catch up.

"Get away," Dalah said. "We're talking about girl stuff."

Vonlai fell a few steps behind but didn't let them get too far ahead. After all this time, Vonlai's mother still insisted that Dalah never go anywhere alone, and Vonlai sensed why. The bad omen always came—his twitching right eye—after crossing paths with Tiger Tong.

Dalah turned around to see if Vonlai was still tailing

her. He pretended not to see her. It was easier to stay near her if he acted like he didn't care where she was.

As he walked, he examined the elephant. Every detail was exact, from the wrinkled skin to the pointed tusks to the angled tail seemingly in motion to swat away flies. Vonlai thought about the old man's words—about parasites rotting your brain—and wondered how many minds, including his own, had already been ruined by doubt.

Chapter
12

July 1982

Meh lay in bed, her shirt pulled up and a wet cloth on her stomach, another one covering her face. Her legs were sprawled out in a careless position. She used to smack Dalah's thighs for the same undignified behavior, but as the months wore on, Meh woke up this way more days than not.

"Are you sick, Meh? I could go to the medical building and ask for some pills," Vonlai offered.

Meh laughed an unfamiliar laugh. The sound of it spread through him like hot tar, bits of gravel grazing his veins.

"There is no medicine for what ails me," she said. "Now go on to school and leave me be."

Vonlai backed away from the bed as Meh lay, her eyes

dull, half smiling at the ceiling. He knew it couldn't be the womanly affliction. This mood came too often. And it wasn't malaria—she didn't have the fever and the tremors and the vomiting—but he almost wished it were. That way, it would at least have a name, and here in Na Pho, maybe there'd be medicine. Or he could sneak Meh's money and try to buy it from the Thai villagers outside the gates.

Vonlai poured a cup of water and downed it. He filled it again and tried to hand it to Meh. "Maybe this'll help."

"Boy, are you planning to show up late to school and disrupt class?"

"Just go," Dalah said. "You can't help her. She'll get better when we get out of this place—if we don't die first." Dalah sat on the bed's edge, a plait of hair draped over her shoulder. She poked a chopstick through the mass, trying to separate a tangle. "I don't know why I bother. The shampoo this place gives us might as well be floor polish the way it gunks up my hair."

Vonlai knew his sister well enough to understand that when the spirits held Meh's good cheer captive, Dalah's concern brought out the worst in her. She refused to talk about a future that may never come, and complaints came easier for her. Vonlai ached at seeing his sister restless and worried. Even so, her constant grumbling buzzed in his ears and went unchecked with Pah assisting the JVA for most of the day. Vonlai was happy to disappear behind the

95

walls of school, even with no breakfast.

Inside the little room, though, the heat was worse with all the students crammed in, but Miss Chada, with that light in her eyes, brought Vonlai a whole new perspective of the world. He sat captivated, his mind soaking up the ideas that were so different from what he learned in Laos.

Under the Pathet Lao, teachers talked about the evils of the outside world. How American women were dishonorable and wore short skirts and tight pants to show off their skin. And how American doctors, greedy Capitalists, would never administer treatment to people with no money, no matter how sick you were. Those same lessons had been played out on the radio, scenarios depicting women begging help for their dying children only to be turned away because they were poor. Vonlai's stomach sank under the weight of that memory.

But Miss Chada smiled when she spoke of the free world and told a far different story of America. A place where jobs were plentiful, and anyone could have a nice place to live and even their own cars, as long as they worked hard. She made sure any student who was interested had time to understand the lessons. She never ridiculed anyone who got confused, or smacked their ears when they made a mistake. And she never pressured those who nodded off because their empty bellies left them listless.

Vonlai absorbed her discussions of governments where

people vote and have jobs, countries that encouraged education and free thinking. She spoke of trade and explorers and advances in technology. Her gestures and face were rich with enthusiasm. Her voice rose and fell like music. Vonlai could barely sit still, his whole body tingling at the prospect of modern equipment, elections, new goods, and marketplaces teeming with activity. His fascination with the outside world extended to Miss Chada's life. He waited until class was dismissed and loitered near the door after the children left.

"What is it?" Miss Chada asked.

"Meh wouldn't like me asking, but I wonder about you."

"Wonder about what?"

"How did you become a teacher? Is the world out there really like you say it is? I mean, the Pathet Lao lied all the time, I just don't know. Where do you go when you leave here?"

"Whoa, slow down. One thing at a time." Miss Chada patted the bench beside her and Vonlai sat down.

"First off, I'm a volunteer from Thailand. I'll be here one more month, until this term ends, then I'll return to Bangkok to finish my education at the university there."

Her smile comforted Vonlai, but he already felt a sense of loss. Miss Chada was a dazzling face amid all the gloom, but she'd said one more month—that's it. Bile rose in his throat as Vonlai realized she would probably be out of this place, taking her light with her, long before he was.

And he remembered Meh lying on the bed. He wouldn't reveal private family details to Miss Chada, but Dalah had said Meh would get better only when they left Na Pho. He looked at his teacher. She didn't make him feel stupid or curse him for being insolent. She just waited and let him sit next to her without any sense of impatience.

Miss Chada knew so much about the world, so Vonlai took a breath and asked her a question. "Maybe you can tell me." His eyes darted to the door, where Noy and other dirty toddlers with runny noses peeked in. "How long will my family be here?"

She swept a piece of hair off Vonlai's forehead. Her fingers felt like freshly set custard, still warm but creamy and smooth. He caught a scent of her sweet perfume. A wall of emotion crashed into him, and his eyes filled with tears. The fragrance reminded Vonlai of a time when he was very young, before the war ended, when Meh would paint Dalah's fingernails a shiny pink while singing softly. *Beautiful girl, with fingers long and straight, fresh and young like new bamboo.* Vonlai had begged to be pampered, too, and Meh squeezed her perfumed lotion into his tiny hand and helped him rub it in soft circles all along his legs.

"Vonlai, you're very bright," Miss Chada said. "And I'm glad you're not afraid to ask questions, but you know I don't have that answer."

"But I want to see for myself the outside world you talk about. I don't even know which country I should invite into my dreams."

"Is your father an educated man? A farmer? Or did he serve in the military?"

"He was schooled in France. He was an architect."

Vonlai waited for a response, but Miss Chada said nothing.

"What?" Vonlai asked. "What can you tell me?"

"I don't have a crystal ball, Vonlai, but with civil servants like your father, the UNHCR tries to place them in the countries where they received their training. But France is tightening its belt. So many refugees put a strain on countries. Can you understand? It's a difficult scenario all the way around."

"I understand. And I'd rather go to America, anyway. They have the tallest skyscrapers in the world."

"Yes, they do."

Vonlai didn't want to ask any more questions. Dalah had heard how military families got the spots in America first. Miss Chada had told him the truth about France. He'd learned enough for the day, and he wanted to check on Meh, even though he knew he couldn't make her better. "Thank you, Miss Chada. You smell good. I'll be back tomorrow."

Miss Chada placed her hands together and bowed her head slightly toward Vonlai to show him respect as if he were an adult. "I know you will."

Chapter
13

Vonlai held a stick firm while Kavin tied a strip of rubber around the prongs. Kavin was the best at crafting sling-shots, making sure the strip was the perfect length to suit the shooter's arm. For the younger kids, he made the strips a little too long so they couldn't shoot one another's eyes out but could still find their warrior pride in lobbing rocks at lizards.

The evening sky mimicked a floating bouquet, a feast of red, plum, and orange orchids drifting in a slow current. The air was cool and light, and it lifted Vonlai's spirits. He and Kavin were at the far end of camp, away from the flurry of activity around the water station. Vonlai didn't want to be home by dark to wither in their tiny room.

"Let's have another round of target practice," Vonlai said.

"Not much light left," Kavin answered, testing the

tension on his newest sling.

"Look there." Vonlai pointed to the roof of a metal storage shed. "See that bent corner? It's reflecting the last bit of sun onto that pile of boxes."

"Good eye," Kavin said, and he gathered up the cans they'd brought to stack in a pyramid on the boxes.

"You go first." Vonlai said. "No pressure or anything."

Kavin exaggerated his hunter stance and made a show of drawing back the sling. He let out a warrior cry and knocked the top can away with barely a clatter. "Top that, Little Brother. No pressure."

Vonlai took a breath, pulled back the sling, steadied his hand, and let his rock fly, but he hit a bottom can. The targets came crashing down.

"Remind me to steer clear of you when you're hunting," Kavin said.

"I had dust in my eye."

"Nurse! Nurse! Hunter afflicted with a sorry excuse."

Vonlai plopped down on his back. "Look. First star." He aimed his slingshot at the sky. "Wish I could hurl myself up there and get out of this place."

Kavin sat down next to him and scooped up a handful of dirt. He held his palm out flat so the breeze could blow wisps of it away. "You can wish anything you want."

There was nothing to say after that. There were only

dreams. And memories. Vonlai rested his head on his hands and let his mind wander back to Laos. He and Khom had shooting contests, too. Khom could hit hard, but his aim was terrible. Vonlai was usually spot-on but never hurt anything with his lobbing shots. One day, a vicious squawking caught their attention. A neighbor's male turkey had a female pinned to the ground, pecking, poking, and scratching her.

"Why does she just sit there and take it?" Vonlai had asked.

"Survival of the species." Khom pulled the slingshot out of his pocket.

"Shoot his wing," Vonlai said. "That'll get him off her."

Khom had closed one eye. Point. Pull. Ping. The rock sailed right over the flock.

"You aimed too high again," Vonlai said. "Now move out of the way and let me show you how to pop it."

Vonlai pulled the sling back, aimed low, and sent his rock sailing. It grazed the dirt a foot in front of the bobbing bird, then bounced up to knock it square in the head. Khom punched Vonlai's shoulder. "Um, you missed your target."

That turkey flopped right over like a bowling pin and convulsed in the dirt. The female trotted off.

"Oh, crap!" Vonlai said.

"Oh, crap is right," Khom said. "Run for your life!"

The two split up and tore through hidden paths. Vonlai made it home in record time, but soon enough, the man's whole family came knocking. Vonlai cowered in a back room and tried to quiet his thumping heart, but he heard the man talking to Meh. Word had it that her boy had shot his bird. And it was dead.

"No wonder you came home early, dummy," Dalah had said. "You're going to get it good."

Meh paid the man the value of his livestock, then came hunting for Vonlai, a switch tight in her hand. His backside was sore for days, and even though he suffered at the shame he caused his mother, he would always have bragging rights on Khom. Master Turkey Killer, his friend had called him.

Vonlai shook his head to shove away the thoughts of a home and friend he'd never see again, and he smacked his ears to make sure the memory didn't creep back in. Just then, he felt a kick on his leg and thought Kavin was rousing him, but he opened his eyes and recognized the outline of Meh hovering over him against the deep purple sky. "Do you know what time it is?"

Vonlai scrambled to his feet. "I forgot."

Meh grabbed Vonlai's slingshot and smacked him on the ear with it. "Forgot what? That we're in a refugee camp with people whose minds get darker each day they wake up and smell the same foul air?"

Vonlai couldn't help but think Meh was one of those people. Her mood rose and fell like ocean waves, and he worried she'd drown under the weight of the water.

She flung Vonlai's slingshot away. "You'll only get yourself in more trouble with that thing. Kavin, you should get home, too."

"Yes, ma'am. I'll be on my way shortly."

Vonlai trailed after Meh, and they soon crossed paths with Tiger Tong. "Pleasant evening to you," the guard said. He was headed toward Kavin.

Vonlai fell back a few steps. Meh didn't bother turning around to check on him. He could hear the guard's gritty voice badgering Kavin, and then he heard a snap, the breaking of wood, and he knew Kavin's slingshot was gone, too.

Chapter
14

Vonlai watched the full moon shrink with each passing night, till nothing but a sliver was left and the sky lost its glow. Wednesdays were a blessing. The meat trucks roared into camp, and the energy in Na Pho swelled so thick, it wrapped around you like a hug from a long-lost friend. Next to the mail trucks that delivered traces of the outside world or a bit of money from loved ones, nothing restored the good cheer among family and neighbors more than the meat trucks.

Pah clapped his hands. "Okay, now, put on your loose pants. We're getting fat tonight!"

"Can I go collect our share this time?" Vonlai asked. "I'll come straight back."

"The fire pit's full of ash," Meh said. "Clean it out, scrub the pots, and go."

Vonlai and Dalah jumped up. They grabbed a bucket

and spoon and raced outside. Vonlai filled the bucket with ash and ran to dump it in a stinking latrine hole. Dalah spooned heaps into the hand-dug wastewater trough that stretched alongside the barracks.

"Now. Get the pots," Dalah ordered, squatting to fill a tub with water.

"You get 'em, bossy," Vonlai said.

"Do you want to eat or argue?"

"Good point." Vonlai tiptoed behind her, snuck a handful of ash, and sprinkled it on her head. Dalah swatted her hair as if a fly had perched there. Vonlai stifled a giggle as he imagined her later discovering her new shade of hair—gritty old woman gray.

He fetched an armload of pots from the side of the front step. "I still don't see why you couldn't carry them."

"Soap," Dalah called, pointing to their supply table. "Because I'm training you to be a gentleman."

"You're training yourself to be a nag."

"Shut up and scrub."

By the time they were done, they skipped going to the truck site and went straight to Savat's. The line was already formed.

"Savat, please," a man said. It was Pasong again, the beggar. "Please, let me get my share first. My wife grows weary suckling our new baby and she needs her strength."

Vonlai heard a shuffling somewhere ahead of him in line. He craned his neck so he could see over the people standing in front of him.

"Now, Pasong," Savat said. "You wouldn't want to cut in front of Colonel, would you?"

Pasong stepped aside and put a hand on the shoulder of the old man with a limp. "No, of course not."

Colonel nodded his thanks to Pasong, collected his share, and scuffled behind Savat's cutting table to his barracks.

Vonlai closed his eyes a second to keep the soothing vision inside, shielded from the dusty ugliness like a possum in his mama's pouch. Such a small act of kindness—letting Colonel go first—but it counted. In Na Pho, there was nothing else to offer but small things.

Back at their fire pit, Vonlai squatted next to Meh to watch her prepare their meal. She laid a knife across the bird and hit the top edge with her palm, smashing through bone. She tossed the chopped-up parts in the pot and hammered away at papaya with her mortar and pestle.

"Fish sauce," she said.

Vonlai handed her the bottle and she dribbled it in. He watched her tiny arm muscles, obvious now with no fat to conceal them, bulge with each blow of the pestle. The scent of fresh papaya and the pungent tang of fish sauce splattered into the air with each whack.

Tonight, Vonlai would be a drumstick shy of being

full, but the hunger would return in a couple days once the meat ran out. He thought of Colonel, and what a meager portion one man must be allotted.

"Do we have room for one more tonight?" Vonlai asked.

"One more what? A chicken?" Meh asked. "Boy, if you can produce a chicken, there's room in this pot."

"No, I mean a person."

Meh stopped pounding and pointed her pestle around their cook site. "There's plenty of dirt to sit on." She swiped her forearm across her brow and started the steady beating again. "I suppose that means there's room for one more as long as they let me cook up their share so I can pretend I splurged at the market."

Vonlai stood, dusted off his hands, and walked past half a building's length of barracks.

The old man sat on his step, his feet in a shallow tub half full of water, and scrubbed between his toes. Various shades of purple scars, slightly curved and no longer than a thumb, slashed Colonel's ankles all the way around. Vonlai could barely stand the sight of them, they were so severe.

"Have you eaten yet, Uncle?" Vonlai asked.

Without looking up, Colonel answered. "No. My driver hasn't arrived to chauffeur me to the restaurant yet."

"Will you come by our place? My mother could add your meat to her pot and spare you the trouble of cooking."

"Mighty fine idea, boy. Grab that bowl there."

Vonlai reached for it, a banana leaf covering the contents. His wrist bent under the unexpected weight, and a chicken—a whole chicken, wings and all—tumbled out! It rolled across the walkway and gathered a coating of dust.

"Oh, Colonel! I beg forgiveness. I didn't know it would be so heavy."

"No matter. It'll clean up fine." Colonel dumped his foot water into the stagnant trough. He grabbed a large bowl, poured in a bit of water, and washed off the chicken. "There. Good as new. Mind carrying it for me?"

As they walked back toward Vonlai's fire pit, men passed the pair and greeted the old man with broad smiles. "Evening, Colonel. Got a new recruit?"

"What's for dinner tonight, Colonel? Got a chef on duty, do you?"

"Uncle," Vonlai said, hesitating before he finished his thought, "why do people call you Colonel?"

"I served in the Royal Lao Army."

"You did?" Vonlai blurted, his mouth dropping open.

"I did. Many of these men here served under me. Fought alongside Americans to try to defeat the Pathet Lao. They were really just boys themselves then, not much older than you, I suspect."

Vonlai was too stunned to say anything else. No wonder Savat gave Colonel as much chicken as he gave a family of four. But how could this withered, unsteady man have led so many soldiers? What had happened to break his body down so mercilessly?

Meh saw the two of them coming. Vonlai was happy to see her face lift a little, even if it was only a show for guests. She pressed her hands together, fingertips pointing skyward, and raised them to her face. *"Sabai Di,"* she greeted the old man.

"Sabai Di," Colonel said. "Your son has invited me to dinner. I won't burden you, I hope."

Meh turned over a crate for Colonel to sit on. "I'm happy to do it, Uncle," she said, gesturing for Dalah to bring him a cup of water.

When the soup was done, Pah helped Colonel position himself on the bamboo mat that covered a bit of ground. Meh ladled the elder his serving first while Dalah and Vonlai waited from their spot a fair distance off to the side, politely outside the circle of adults.

"Mmm. Delicious," Colonel told Meh, slurping his dinner. "You do quite a job with a skinny bird and some water."

"It's only because you were generous to add your share to the pot," Meh said. "We thank you."

Vonlai held his cup close to his mouth and scooped in the broth, peering over the top to study Colonel and his warped ankle.

"It's ugly, isn't it, child?" Colonel called to Vonlai.

Vonlai coughed and choked at getting caught staring. Dalah elbowed his ribs for being rude.

"Uncle," Pah said, "my apologies for the boy."

"It's fine. He should see," Colonel said, stretching his foot into open space. "We can't ever close our eyes to the Pathet Lao's treatment of us."

"You were in seminar camp?" Pah asked.

"It might as well have been the end of the earth. I shouldn't be alive today. Half the people there died slow, miserable deaths." Colonel rubbed his hands, up and down, up and down on his thighs as he spoke. "Sister, Brother, I must apologize. This is not pleasant dinner conversation."

"No, please go on," Pah said. "You're right. History doesn't change just because we fear the truth. We'll hear your story."

Colonel took a sip of water then folded his hands together, his fingers locked, before he spoke again. "So many were sick with disease and malnutrition. Starving if they couldn't catch rats or grasshoppers or tadpoles to eat. Insane and dying in underground jails ripe with waste and blood. It was the Pathet Lao's way to kill us, and the world knew nothing of it. I escaped when I was working the fields. I knew the country-side well, as my boyhood home was up north. But others surely died because I stole my freedom back. I'd seen it happen before. Prisoners falsely accused of helping people get out. Beaten to within inches of their lives by authorities to set an example, then finished off by fellow detainees under order from the guards. Other men who tried to escape were caught and shot in front of everyone. So many are still there. So many are dying right now."

"Colonel," Vonlai said. He had stood to come closer, unable to sit and endure the horrors that blasted his chest so hard he couldn't breathe. "Did you have family? You're here alone. Are they still there?"

Colonel closed his eyes. "No, boy. They are not there."

Pah put a hand on Vonlai to keep him from asking more questions.

"These scars," Colonel said, rubbing his ankles. "They put me in leg stocks. A fellow prisoner accused me of being a reactionary."

"But how?" Vonlai blurted. "How could he do that to you?"

"He is not to blame. You must understand. The Communists thrived on creating paranoia. We lived in constant fear of death by denunciation. If you had no transgressions to report against a fellow inmate, a machete was thrust under your chin. But a few minutes of daylight or an extra bit of rice—rancid rice with mice droppings that reeked of diesel oil—were rewards for making up lies about other prisoners. It gave the Pathet Lao an excuse to kill us. I was beaten while still in shackles and fell off my sleeping platform. When I landed, the stocks shattered my ankle. Death hung around every corner. Every day we feared would be our last."

Vonlai had no stomach for food. He dumped his uneaten rice back in the pot. Silent tears spilled down Dalah's cheeks. And the sadness on Meh's face covered an undercurrent of something: Shame? Embarrassment over her own gloom? She managed a slight smile, a show of empathy.

Colonel shifted on the mat. He was clearly in pain, but he stayed put. "The Communists' treatment of the Laotian people was inhuman. And it continues as we sit here tonight, free enough to share this feast among friends." Colonel looked at Vonlai and held his gaze. "The only way to restore my dignity as a man is to speak the truth."

Chapter
15

August 1982

Vonlai would complete his sixth-grade year at one o'clock, and the monotonous days ahead offered no hope of getting out of Na Pho. Vonlai wished he could turn back the clock so he could stay in school, even if it meant relearning lessons he'd already heard and told to himself many times over.

He woke before anyone else and walked to the camp's front gate before his last day of school started. The dreams in his mind were slipping away. Vonlai had to see for himself that life outside Na Pho still existed. Just beyond the gates, Thai villagers were setting up shop, their carts full of cigarettes, liquor, beef jerky, baskets, shampoo, bags of coconut juice, and blocks of ice for any Lao refugee willing to pay for such a luxury.

"You, boy!" a vendor called. "You have money to spend?"

Vonlai shook his head.

"Come on, skinny bones, I have fried bananas. Your pants are sagging—you must have *some* change in there weighing you down."

Vonlai turned his pockets out to show the man. "See? No money to buy anything."

"All right, then. Move along," the vendor said. "I've got to make my living, son."

Vonlai started back home. The morning was quiet, and the dust had not yet whipped up. People milled through camp, men with their shirts rolled up to their armpits, women squatting at makeshift food stands, their mortars and pestles grinding papaya and lime, or their knives slicing tiny strips of beef to dry for jerky.

Vonlai could barely handle the aroma, it made his stomach ache so much. He was hungry, but not starving—the UN delivered just enough food to keep people from dying—but he wanted flavor.

When he returned, Meh was awake. She leaned over the cook fire, arranging scraps of wood. "I don't like you going off by yourself."

"We've been here four months," Vonlai said. "Nothing's ever happened."

Meh didn't answer, looking too tired to challenge him.

Vonlai filled her cooking pot with water. "We have a little money, right? Why can't we buy something, Meh, just once, from the market outside? We eat the same thing every day."

"When we start to die, we'll buy something. Do you see Colonel wasting his money on frivolous desires? We could all learn something from that man. I'm saving our money so we can get ourselves set up in America, or wherever they send us."

Meh's words soothed Vonlai. She had plans—a vision of a new home outside Na Pho—or she wouldn't be hoarding the money.

Vonlai stepped behind the shower screen, dribbled cupfuls of water over his head, and worked up a lather from the one remaining soap chip. The bubbles washed over him as he let his mind wander.

He saw himself standing in an American city, brand-new Nike shoes on his feet and skyscrapers shooting up around him. He'd be free to look into any store window he wanted. Pah would buy him a brand-new soccer ball. Or a new notebook with crisp white paper. Or a Coca-Cola he could have all to himself. And best of all . . . it would be snowing. Swathes of clean, soft snow would brighten the city, streetlights sparkling in winter's mirror, just like he'd seen in the forbidden magazines he and Khom snuck from street vendors in Laos.

"Vonlai, enough!" Meh yelled as she poured rice in the pot. A puddle just outside his shower platform had filled up. The overflow veined out across the dirt, and the sludgy trail trickled under Meh's feet. "That trench needs to be dug out again."

"I'll be done in a minute," Vonlai said.

"Until then, my feet get muddied."

With soap in his hair, Vonlai wrapped a towel around his waist and grabbed an ax. He was relieved to see Meh notice the mess. Her nagging comforted him, compared to the silence that made her fade away. He squatted to chip away caved dirt, and the waterway opened so the puddle could drain away.

Pah stood in the doorway, arms stretched skyward, and spoke through a yawn. "Looks like you have things handled, son. Maybe I should stay in bed."

As time wore on, the JVA didn't need Pah's services so frequently, and he spent more time sleeping away the wait or talking with men about the Laos of their childhoods. If there were fewer refugees being admitted to Na Pho, did that mean the world was shutting its doors to the homeless? With his feet sunk in Na Pho mud, Vonlai lost his vision of America. It was only a fantasy on the other side of the world, and he was no closer to getting there than he was when they crossed the Mekong River. *Maybe Pah should go back to sleep*, Vonlai thought. *What reason was there to get out of bed? Come tomorrow, with school finished, I won't have one.*

"Good morning, Aunt," Kavin called to Meh. "Came to beg some coconut milk off you."

"Coconut milk, huh? Your imagination is rich, Kavin," Meh said. "Why don't you watch my rice and imagine it to be a pot full of oxtail soup?" Meh left for the latrines.

"What are you lurking around here for?" Vonlai asked, back behind the shower screen.

"Dalah awake yet?" Kavin asked, shifting his weight to see inside.

"No. She's a slug."

"Let's get a game started before the sun gets too high, then."

"Can't," Vonlai said, dipping another cup of water from the barrel. "Got school." He wiped the soap from under his arms.

"Hey, big man," Kavin teased. "You finally sprouted some pit hair."

"I *am* thirteen," Vonlai said, puffing up his chest. "I'm nearly a man."

"Pardon me, then, Uncle. What about down below?"

"I bet you want to know!" Vonlai said. "I thought you liked my sister anyway."

Kavin reached past the shower wall to punch Vonlai's arm. "Seriously, Little Brother, you can't call yourself a man if your salami's bald. Better shave what you got. It'll grow back twice as thick."

"Really?" Vonlai asked. "You tried this yourself and it worked?"

"Guaranteed. I'll teach you everything you need to know. Now forget about school so we can play."

Vonlai shook his head no.

"Come on," Kavin said. "America already has a president. What do you want from school? Besides, it's only one day. What are you going to learn in one day that'll make your life so much better?"

"You don't understand."

"I don't understand? So you take me for a lamebrain now? Think you're smarter than me?"

"I didn't say that," Vonlai said.

"What, then?" Kavin asked.

"I'm not a quitter. That's all."

Kavin fell back a step as if someone had punched his chest. "Well, good for you, but I'm not the son of an architect who rubbed shoulders with Americans, either." His lips twitched as he spoke. "You know how many times we've been passed over for interviews, Vonlai? Do you? What country wants an illiterate farmer and all his uneducated sons?" Kavin threw a towel at Vonlai and started to leave. "Go on to school, you punk! Maybe one day you'll come back to save me—if you can recognize me in my old man skin!"

Vonlai stood, rigid as dried-out rice, as Kavin ran off.

He felt the last bit of water trail down his arms and drip off each fingertip. Meh came back around the corner, and he turned away to grab the scoop. Vonlai held his breath as he dumped a final cupful of water on his head to camouflage his tears.

Chapter
16

Miss Chada brought coconut cookies. She tore open the pink foil and set one in front of each student. Grains of sugar on top sparkled like diamond chips. Vonlai pressed his tongue on the cookie to soak up the sweet without biting it. He wanted to hold it awhile to make it last.

"You dummy!" a fifth grader said. "It's not gonna grow if you water it with your spit. Eat it already, or I'll do it for you!"

"Good things come to those who are patient," Miss Chada said in English. "Vonlai has learned this well, don't you think, Sert?" And she put a second cookie in Vonlai's hand.

Roars of protest rattled the room.

"Now, now," Miss Chada said as she gave the rest of the sixth graders a second cookie. "We need to wish our friends well on their last day. And treat them with respect, for they are graduates now."

"Miss Chada," Vonlai asked, "may I have the foil wrapper, please?"

"Of course."

He ate half of the first cookie, his jaws moving in slow, exaggerated circles for Sert's benefit. He left the rest sitting on the edge of his desk in plain view.

As good as it tasted, the sugar, so foreign to Vonlai's system, didn't sit well in his stomach.

Kavin was right. There was nothing to be learned in a day that would make his life better. It was worse, in fact, because he had insulted his friend and caught a glimpse of his future.

Vonlai had seen other people get out of the refugee camp. Their eyes were bright, even as they tried to conceal their smiles. They knew what it was like to watch others before them pack up and leave, their happiness mixed with sorrow for those who had to stay. Vonlai had always wished it were his family going instead, but he always believed his time would come soon.

Kavin didn't. He'd been at Na Pho nearly as long as Dalah's friend, Jun. Almost four years. Four years of getting passed over. Like Kavin had said, not everyone had connections to America that would push along the process. Others didn't have the proper documents—and no one to vouch for them—to prove they hadn't supported the Communists in any small way.

Vonlai finished the first cookie and tucked the second one into the wrapper. He folded the foil over and tried to rub out the wrinkles, but instead, he broke the cookie. He rolled his finger over the tiniest crumbs and pushed the bigger pieces back together. Maybe Kavin wouldn't mind, even if it was falling apart.

When school finished, Vonlai barely managed to mutter a "thank you" to Miss Chada. He'd had his fill of good-byes and didn't need any motivating words about the value of learning. He only needed opportunity, and that she could not give him. But today the meat trucks would come, and Meh would have soup for him tonight—chicken or fish. Either one would be perfect.

Vonlai ran to the soccer fields to find Kavin. He'd invite him to dinner and give him the cookie he'd saved. But Kavin wasn't there. He wasn't in the latrines. Vonlai waited, watching the shadows shift. He felt a tap on his shoulder to go into the game.

"Your turn, Skeleton Boy."

It wasn't Kavin, but still, Vonlai's legs tingled and he couldn't sit still. He tore off his shirt and used it to bundle the foiled-wrapped cookie like a newborn. If not, a mini mob would discover it, and it'd pass from hand to hand until not a crumb was left.

Vonlai ran into the game, and after only a few minutes, Tiger Tong stood at the sidelines, his eyes tracking him.

Does he expect me to come out already? Vonlai wondered. He ignored Tong and kept running.

A teammate passed him the ball. Vonlai had a fair shot at the goal. He maneuvered around an opponent and felt the pounding of legs behind him. As he sped up, Vonlai winced as the sting of a foot on his shin sent him flying. Vonlai landed on his shoulder. He rolled over, gasping for air. Tiger Tong stood over him, a leg on each side of his chest so he couldn't sit up. And Tong wore no shirt, either.

"We're on the same team," Vonlai rasped.

"Where's your sister and her boyfriend?" the guard asked, the sun directly behind him so that Vonlai saw nothing but black for a face.

"Why do you want to know?"

Tong kicked a heel into Vonlai's side and bent down over his face. "I ask the questions, you little mutt. So do me a favor, will you?"

Vonlai didn't move.

The heel dug in deeper. "Did you hear me? I said do me a favor, like a good little homeless boy."

A spray of Tong's spit fell on Vonlai's face. He nodded.

"Tell your sister I miss her." Tong scraped his heel across the ground, sending a cloud of dirt into Vonlai's face. Tong stepped on his fingers before returning to the game.

Vonlai rolled over and sat up. Nobody came to help

him. How could they with Tong still on the field? Vonlai's shoulder, side, and fingers throbbed. But worse still was the cold that crawled along his skin, coating each pore with dread.

On the walk home, Vonlai carried his rolled-up shirt, careful not to let the cookie slip out.

Meh stood leaning against their barracks, her lower half lit by the sun reaching under the awning. It split her in two at the waist. An orange glow pierced the dark that hid her upper body.

Ten steps closer and Vonlai could see—Meh was smoking a cigarette.

"Where'd you get that?" he asked, noticing Meh's money pouch hanging outside her shirt.

Meh didn't answer, and Vonlai knew she'd gone to the Thai merchants to buy cigarettes.

Vonlai looked inside the cooking pot. "Why isn't the meat cooking yet?"

Meh was deaf to him. She sucked again on the cigarette and the end glowed red.

"Figure it out," Dalah said.

His stomach lurched.

The rumble of meat trucks. Vonlai hadn't heard it today. And there were no squealing children, rushing to the center of camp. There was no chicken for soup. There was no fish.

"Meh, what are we going to eat this week?"

"More rice," Pah said. "And we still have vegetables."

"Yeah, this refugee camp is so much better than living in Laos," Dalah said, scrubbing her sarong in a pot of muddy water.

"Meh, will the trucks come tomorrow then?" Vonlai said.

Meh dragged on her cigarette, looking at nothing.

"I'm hungry, Meh," Vonlai said. "I want some meat. My stomach is a raisin, and you spend money on tobacco instead of food!"

Meh threw her cigarette on the ground and pounded her fist on their metal barracks. "*Oi!* If I could cry anymore, I'd let you drink my tears! Get a knife and cut my neck," Meh screamed, rubbing circles over her heart. "You can swallow my blood till your stomach overflows!"

Meh yanked the pouch hanging from her neck, snapping the strap. She tore into it and tossed Vonlai a handful of coins. "Go buy peppers so we can eat. Get a tomato if they have it. We'll have a feast on a couple dabs of nam jeel!"

Dalah couldn't get up fast enough, but Vonlai stood there, money in one hand—way too much for what Meh told him to buy—and Kavin's coconut cookie still rolled into his shirt in the other hand.

"Come on," Dalah whispered. "Before she changes her mind."

I've really done it now, Vonlai thought. His complaining had stripped Meh of her hope, made her willing to waste the money she was saving for America. Why was he so greedy? He wasn't going to die. He could eat rice another week. Everyone else had to as well.

Skeleton Boy—that's me, he thought. *Stupid shell of a person. Wanting. Whining. Greedy. Empty.*

Dalah pulled his arm. "Come on!"

"Go on, son," Pah said, dragging a wet towel down his neck. "We could all use a taste of something spicy tonight."

Meh was inside, sprawled on the bed, wailing.

Vonlai fingered the money in his hand. He turned to go, but not before slamming his shirt into the dirt. He watched the cookie roll out, its unfolding foil crackling like a dying fire.

Chapter
17

Vonlai woke in the middle of the night, his gut quaking from the peppers he'd eaten. The fire in his mouth had filled the hole in his heart, but too many months had passed since spice was a regular part of his diet, and his stomach suffered the burn.

He remembered to grab the water bucket as he hurried to the latrines. On his first trip, he didn't think he'd make it in time. He had to tear off a piece of his shirt to clean himself, and Meh would be none too pleased to see he'd wasted good clothes.

The stall was pitch-black. Vonlai couldn't tell where to slap at the buzzing mosquitoes, and they tore into him. He poured water over his backside and rushed out, but he didn't want to wake Meh by crawling in bed—again. Her sleep was not a peaceful one.

Vonlai left the toilet bucket by the shower screen and

started walking. His stomach wasn't going to let him sleep, anyway, so he trekked up the hill to the soccer field. Out in the open, away from the trees and human smell sardined into the barracks, the mosquitoes weren't as thick. Vonlai lay flat in the field. The dirt, worn fine by pounding feet and no longer holding the sun, cooled his back.

Far-off voices, slurred with drink, wandered to him. Vonlai recognized Kavin's laugh. It rose in a careless crescendo while others responded with shushes. Clinking bottles accompanied the twinkling stars overhead. They were so bright, the sky looked milky.

Vonlai heard a whimper. He held his breath to listen. It was a cry of pain. Almost a plea. And it was much closer than Kavin and his friends, but with noises in the night bouncing off metal barracks, Vonlai couldn't tell from which direction it came.

Maybe someone was having a nightmare, Vonlai thought. He sat up. A rustling of brush came from somewhere in the shrub. Past the soccer goalposts, maybe? Did the cry come from an injured animal? Was it a desperate bobcat stalking his waif of a body for an easy meal?

Vonlai heard a smack and then nothing. No rustle. No whimper. No more protest.

A chill ran down Vonlai's neck as he admitted to himself the sound was human. Someone scared and suffering. An unwilling girl with no choice. Vonlai forced the violent image out of his mind and wished he could believe it was only a drunk who'd lost his way in the brush, stepped on a rock, and passed out.

His body was fixed on the ground the way a petrified baby clings to his mother. And then Tong's words clawed at Vonlai's heart. *Tell your sister I miss her.*

He wasted no time running home. A slice of gray broke up the black sky. People would wake soon.

He tiptoed into his room. The sound of sleep stirred the stagnant air. It was Dalah's sleep, as well as Pah's and Meh's. *Good,* Vonlai thought as he let out a breath. It grazed his parched throat. But what about the girl in the brush? He'd done nothing—except run away.

Vonlai reached for the water and swigged it straight from the jug, but when he set it back on the crate, he knocked over the tiny elephant Colonel had given him so many weeks ago.

"*Sshh,*" Vonlai whispered to the wooden creature. He set it upright and ran his hand over its back and down the sides. He could feel variations in the wood where the elephant's muscles were strongest. Vonlai hadn't noticed that with his eyes. *How did Colonel do that?* Vonlai wondered. *It's just a piece of wood.*

He reached under the bed, grabbed a sheet, and wrapped it around his shoulders to ward off the mosquitoes. Outside, he wandered through camp as early risers began to stir. Was the girl there, her colorless shape one of many shifting against the gray of first light? Kavin wouldn't be one of them. Wasting away the morning in bed was the only way to clear the haze of drink from his mind, and Vonlai couldn't help but wonder if it was his own careless words that made Kavin crave the blur.

With nowhere to go, Vonlai found himself in front of Colonel's room, staring at the closed door. He sat on the porch and covered his head with the sheet.

Vonlai must have slept. His rear was numb and the sun had turned his cover into a white-hot sauna.

"Aha," Colonel said, wrapping his short sarong between his legs and tucking it in around his waist. "I see I have my own pet ghost now. Does the ghost have an appetite for breakfast?" He held out a banana for Vonlai.

Vonlai reached out from the sheet to accept it. He wanted to tear into it, but that would appear greedy. "Can you teach me to carve?"

"Manners, boy. I think that's a lesson that would serve you better."

"I'm sorry, Uncle," Vonlai said, pulling down the peel. "Thank you for the breakfast. I'd like to learn how you do it—how to carve. If it wouldn't burden you, that is."

"Do you have patience?"

"I think so."

"Yes, it's certainly evident," Colonel said. "You were

patient enough to not wake me when you parked on my stoop in the middle of the night, eager for your lesson. Now go show yourself to your mother first. Her heart might fail at the sight of an empty bed."

All day, Vonlai watched the old man carve. He wasn't allowed to touch a knife until he could demonstrate fortitude.

"I won't have your blood on my hands," Colonel said in his gravelly voice, pulling the knife over the wood. "You won't learn much if your eagerness leaves you with a severed thumb."

Vonlai picked up the shavings that dropped in the dirt, some of them razor thin. He held them to his nose to breathe in the scent of possibility, the fresh-cut smell of something being created.

As he watched Colonel work, Vonlai wondered about the man's family. It was the one thing he'd never heard Colonel speak of, except that evening during dinner when he'd said they were not in seminar camp. *Where were they then?* Vonlai tried to slow his surging brain by focusing on Colonel's hands as he cut into the wood. Too much prying would prove he wasn't patient, and that he was insolent by digging into an adult's private business.

Vonlai worked up the nerve to ask one question, the least intrusive. "Uncle, what is your name?"

"You'd do fine to continue calling me Uncle. Or Colonel, if you wish."

"What was it like serving in the Royal Lao Army? Did you fly across the ocean to train in America? What were the clouds like? Did you eat in a restaurant?"

"You ask a string of questions when you don't get an answer to the first? Is that your idea of patience?"

"I'm sorry, Colonel. I'll do better." Vonlai locked his fingers into each other. "Can I try my hand at the carving now? My mouth might stay shut longer if my hands are busy."

Colonel paused to look at Vonlai's face. The man's eyes were soft, Vonlai noticed, and not as old as his broken body made him appear, but they were sad just the same.

"I'd be happy to try something simple," Vonlai said. "Just to feel the power in the knife."

"The power's not in the knife, son. It's here," Colonel said, leaning forward to tap the blade against Vonlai's head. "You've got to start with a vision. The craft can be learned, but it's the vision that can't be taught."

Vonlai made every effort to keep his mouth shut to show his patience.

Colonel handed him the knife. "Yes, then. Something simple. I can see your eagerness to begin is blinding you. Choose a piece of wood."

Colonel dumped the chunks into Vonlai's lap. He

picked up each one, studying them from all angles as he'd seen Colonel do, but no ideas rushed into his head. They all looked like scraps he'd use to start a cook fire.

Vonlai narrowed the stack down to three pieces, praying an idea would come to him. He tried to hold them all at once to scrutinize each piece. He wanted to show Colonel that he had vision, but his mind was as empty as his stomach. He tried to pick up a fourth piece to buy more time, but he bobbled the load. Three pieces landed between his legs, but one rolled on, passing straight between the boundaries of his feet that pointed skyward.

Vonlai tilted his head to look at the piece of wood that had separated itself from the others. His heart tingled a bit, and he knew what he would create.

Chapter
18

After three days sitting with Colonel, listening to the grumbles and groans of a perfectionist teacher, Vonlai finished his first piece. His wrist was swollen, his fingers were numb, and his blisters had finally stopped bleeding, but he was done.

Vonlai held up his handiwork and harumphed at its lopsidedness. It was smaller than he wanted, after he had worked the wood over and over again to make it smooth, but its shape was there, and the patterns were recognizable. He rolled his miniature soccer ball on the ground. Its path, arcing from the imbalance, traced a curved line in the dirt.

"Good work, Vonlai," Colonel said, picking up the ball and rolling it between his palms.

"But it's crooked."

"The simplest things are sometimes the most difficult. The slightest imperfection will show itself in a shape that's expected to be perfect. But the simplest things can also be the most rewarding. This is a good first effort."

Vonlai wanted to race to show Kavin, but he didn't know how to heal the hurt he'd caused. He ran to show Pah and Meh instead, but only Dalah was home. She lay facedown and sobbing on the bed. He hadn't seen her cry like this since they first came to Na Pho.

"What happened?"

Dalah didn't acknowledge him.

Vonlai ran to look for Meh. She was sitting around a neighbor's cook fire sifting through the rice to pick out stones. Tiny hidden pebbles could break your teeth in one bite.

"Meh," Vonlai said, leaning to whisper in her ear. "Something's wrong with Dalah. She's on the bed and won't stop crying."

"Boy, we all wear down like that time and again in this place. It's as certain as the sun rising every day only to sink back behind the earth too soon."

"But she's really bad. Didn't even scream at me to get out. She kept crying like I wasn't even there."

Meh stood up and dusted off her hands.

Vonlai followed her to the barracks and sat in the door-way.

"Daughter, what is it? Are you sick?" Meh ran her hand down the back of Dalah's neck.

137

Dalah curled herself into a ball, shying away from Meh's touch.

Meh's face went white and she pulled her hand away. "Has someone hurt you?" Meh hesitated, then gently touched Dalah's thighs, trying to see between them. "Dalah, did someone lay their hands on you?"

Vonlai's heart burned with thoughts of the whimper he'd heard in the brush the other night. But Dalah had been in bed. He'd seen her there sleeping between Pah and Meh. Did someone get to her at another time? *Tell your sister I miss her.*

Meh pulled soaked strands of hair off Dalah's cheeks. "You have to tell me or I'll send Vonlai after Pah."

Between sobs, Vonlai made out what Dalah was saying. "Jun's family passed their interviews."

Vonlai swallowed hard, but the lump wouldn't go down. Dalah's best friend was leaving. They'd gotten out. A family was waiting to sponsor them in America. Someplace called Minnesota.

Where in the world is Minnesota? Vonlai wondered. But what did it matter? It was in America. Jealousy soaked into him like gasoline poisoning the ground. Why couldn't it have been us? Vonlai cursed at himself for being so selfish. Jun was his friend, too, and he wanted the best for her family. *That's what this place does to you,* he thought. *You only want, want, want for yourself, and anger tears its way up your throat when someone else gets the chance you hoped would be yours.*

Three days later, Jun's parents hugged Pah and Meh good-bye. "Your time will come. We'll pray to our ancestors that it will be soon."

"I'll send you letters," Jun told Dalah. "And pictures, so you can see what's coming your way. I just know you'll get out soon." Jun tried to hug Dalah, but Dalah's arms hung straight at her sides, and she never lifted her chin off her chest to see them leave. Jun was the one crying now. Dalah had no tears left.

Every family who got out of Na Pho and had to say good-bye to their friends said the same thing when they left. *Your turn will come soon.* He'd heard it over and over. And Kavin had been here even longer. How many times had his friend's heart turned on itself, happy for those who were leaving but also breaking for his own fate at being stuck in a place where time didn't matter?

Dalah spent the day in bed, baking inside their metal-wrapped room. Meh ran a wet towel across Dalah's forehead to soak up the sweat, but her gaze stayed fixed on the ceiling.

"You need to eat, Dalah," Meh said. "A broken heart won't be cured by an empty stomach."

Dalah stared, barely blinking.

"Eat, daughter," Meh said.

Dalah shook her head and rolled toward the wall.

"Take her share," Pah said to Vonlai, holding out a cup of rice.

"No way," Vonlai said. "She'll feel better soon. She'll eat it."

Dalah buried a scream inside her throat. It sounded like a dying animal's last effort to fend off a predator.

"Eat it," Pah said quietly to Vonlai. "It'll be hard as rocks by morning."

Vonlai set the bowl in his lap and waited. He hoped Dalah would change her mind. She didn't move, and finally, her breathing turned heavy, and she mumbled in her sleep.

Vonlai finished her rice, but he felt sick afterward. For the first time in Na Pho, his stomach was full, but it was only because his sister's heart was broken.

Chapter
19

By morning, that dank sadness still hovered in the barracks. Dalah's sleeping shirt was soaked through with sweat, but she remained in bed.

Kavin would know how to cheer her up. He was the one sure thing that could bring a smile to Dalah's face. Vonlai ran to Kavin's barracks to tell him. "Jun's left."

"Good for Jun." His expression didn't change as he sat on a crate waiting for the rice pot to boil.

"You still mad at me?"

Kavin threw a stick in the fire pit. "I'm mad at the world, Little Brother. And sometimes it's better if friends don't get in the way."

"Well, Dalah's sick with sadness. She wouldn't even eat."

Kavin winced at the news.

"At first we thought she was hurt," Vonlai said, and then wished he could take it back.

Kavin looked up, ready for a fight. "Hurt how?"

"Never mind. She's not hurt, after all, at least not on her body." Vonlai told no one what Tiger Tong had said about missing Dalah. "But none of us can get her to talk."

"Can I go to her?"

"Why do you think I'm here?"

Kavin headed out, but Vonlai knew Dalah would respond better if he made himself scarce.

He spent the rest of the day following the shade and carving with Colonel, who thumped him on the head every now and then for an errant cut. When Vonlai could almost see his friend's knuckles throb under his papery skin, he feigned fatigue so they could switch to a game of cards. Colonel would never admit to wearing out first.

When Colonel outwitted him with a new magic trick, Vonlai cursed at the old man in French—French words he learned from Colonel himself.

Colonel laughed his throaty chuckle. "Boy, you better stick to what you're good at. You won't be fending off French invaders with *that* pronunciation. Maybe you could pounce on them after they fall down laughing at your language skills!"

Vonlai welcomed the distraction of Colonel's jovial mood, but he still wanted to know more about his life before Na Pho, how he could speak so many languages. Colonel was quick to answer simple questions about his education in France, his training in America where he had learned to speak his third language, English, and his boyhood dream to find the edge of the earth by rowing across the Mekong when he was only six years old.

But Vonlai never asked about Colonel's family. It was the quickest way to lose a carving partner for the day.

"Can you teach me a few English words, Colonel? Tell me about America. I'm in the mood for a dream."

"America," Colonel said in English. *"Land of the free. Home of the brave."* Then he switched back to Lao. "A place where they have special food for dogs."

"What do you mean, special food?"

"Food for dogs that people don't eat. Comes in little cans or big bags. Americans buy it at their market stores."

"You mean Americans don't give their old rice to the dogs?" Vonlai asked, trying to wrap his mind around what a dog would eat other than table scraps.

"Well, Americans don't eat rice every day. Even if they did, they still have a type of food only for dogs. Ground-up meat that people don't eat. *Dog food.*"

"Why can't people eat it if it's meat?"

"Because it's food for dogs. Specially made for puppies. Old dogs. Even fat dogs."

Vonlai let out a laugh. "Fat dogs! Now I know you're teasing! Tell me something that's true."

"Hmmm." Colonel rubbed an ache from his wrist.

"They have a machine that washes dinner plates. A dishwasher. Load them in. Push a button. *Works like magic. Dishes are sparkling clean.*"

"Wow, they think of everything, don't they?"

"They are very, very smart," Colonel said. "I once saw an exercise machine. A stationary bicycle. Americans buy them for their homes so they don't have to go outside to get their muscles moving."

"A bicycle that doesn't move?" Vonlai tried to picture such a thing.

"The pedals move, but the bike stays in one place."

"Unbelievable," Vonlai said, trying to imagine the point of sitting on a bike that goes nowhere. "Spinning the wheels for nothing. I think I've had plenty of that right here in Na Pho."

On the way home, Vonlai passed Kavin's place. He was attaching a wheel to scrap wood he'd hammered together.

"What do you think of my wheelbarrow?" Kavin asked, stretching his shirt up to wipe the sweat off his face. "Noy's been asking for a wagon, but I could only find one wheel."

Vonlai grabbed the handles and gave it a test spin. "It's perfect. Balanced well. I'll carve him some knobs and levers you can attach inside."

"Is that what you've been doing all day? Sitting with

Colonel punishing innocent wood scraps?"

"Ha. Colonel says I have a talent for it. How's Dalah?"

Kavin laid his screwdriver down. "I took her for a long walk. Bought her a coconut drink."

"Meh let her go with you?"

"Who do you think gave me the money? And she warned me not to let her alone. Your sister's better now. She's sleeping."

"Thank you for helping her. None of us could."

"We all help where we can. Like you helping Colonel."

"What do you mean?"

Kavin rubbed a stone across the wheelbarrow's walls, smoothing away splinters. "He's had it rough. Seems he's taken you under his wing."

"What do you know about him?"

"Too much."

"Tell me."

Kavin studied Vonlai's face, sizing him up before going on. "He had a family once. A wife. Two sons. After Colonel was captured, they tried to get on without him, but they could barely feed themselves. The Communists tricked his wife into joining Colonel in seminar camp. They promised to take care of her and the little ones, but it was another lie. She and the boys had to work the fields like everyone else."

Kavin poured himself a cup of water.

"And?" Vonlai asked.

Kavin swished the water around his mouth and spit it in the dirt. "Their spades hacked into land mines and they were all blown to bits."

Chapter
20

When morning came, Meh nudged Vonlai awake. With a grave heart over Colonel's family and a mind heavy with guilt at thinking his own situation was the most dire, Vonlai craved the escape of sleep.

"Go after Dalah," Meh said, pulling Vonlai out of bed. "She's run off before I could even get the water boiling."

Vonlai wiped his eyes, slipped on his flip-flops, and headed out.

He found a group of girls giggling near the soccer field. Dalah was right in the middle, chatting and laughing, but her eyes were swollen and vacant. She saw Vonlai watching her, and she turned her back.

Vonlai recognized these girls. They hung in a tight group and made themselves available to boys, giggling and parading themselves. Most were older than Dalah, at least seventeen or eighteen. One looked to be pregnant, but

Vonlai didn't think she had a husband.

One girl tapped Dalah's shoulder and pointed at Vonlai.

"Get lost," Dalah told him. He ignored her as usual and pretended to discover something fascinating under a nearby rock.

"I said get lost." Dalah crossed her arms over her chest. "I mean it."

"I can be here if I want," Vonlai said. He didn't want to embarrass Dalah by reminding her Meh insisted she not be out alone.

But Dalah wasn't backing down. "Hey, girls, you know any other thirteen-year-old boys who babysit their fifteen-year-old sisters?" They all laughed. "Now get out of here!"

"I thought Kavin cheered you up."

Dalah kicked a heap of dust at Vonlai. "What good was that? I'll only lose him someday, too!"

Vonlai brushed the dust off his hair. "Well, I'm not going."

Dalah's new friend scooped up a handful of gravel and hurled it at Vonlai. "Are your ears full of dirt? Your sister said go!"

Vonlai covered his eyes but cracked his fingers open to watch Dalah. Was she really going to stand there and let these girls—girls she had avoided until today—throw rocks at him?

A feeling of nothingness took over him. Emptiness

bubbled out, an infection that oozed over his skin. Acid coated his tongue.

Jun was gone, but only after four years. Colonel was lonely and broken. Kavin didn't believe in his future. Meh's, and now Dalah's, fluctuating moods were as disturbing as a waking volcano. And Pah's promise of a short stay had been broken long ago.

Vonlai stood up and faced his sister. "You better get used to me tailing you, Dalah! I don't care about these stupid girls you call your friends. We're never getting out of this crappy place—never! And I'm going to follow you every step you take. Then you can watch as my flesh turns black and rots off my bones because no country is ever going to have a place for us!"

Vonlai's throat nearly closed. He thought he would faint. Putting his worry into words gave the fear more power. It took over his body, and he began to sweat and shake, his eyes welling up.

What good was he to Dalah, anyway? A crybaby can't protect his sister, he thought, especially a sister who doesn't want protecting. Vonlai turned to run before anyone saw his tears fall. He ran past the water station and behind the processing building, disappearing into a small grove of trees that lined the edge of camp. He kept running, but there was no escaping this place. Boiling blood pummeled his temples.

A branch snapped his cheek. He tumbled over a rock and landed facedown on the path. Vonlai lay there panting like a dog too exhausted to search for food. The salt from his sorrow burned the fresh cut on his face. Tears kept coming. They rolled off his cheeks and landed on the ground, forming tiny fleeting puddles before being swallowed altogether by Na Pho dirt.

Chapter
21

Vonlai didn't bother getting up from where he fell. He lay sprawled over the ground, motionless, noticing nothing around him. He was numb inside and out, and waited for a reason to move. Nothing came.

Minute by minute, as he started to become aware of the wheeze of his own breath flowing in and out, his heartbeat settled. Parrots sang as they rustled the canopy overhead, hopping from branch to branch. *Had they not been there just a moment before?* Vonlai wondered. How could he have missed their rowdy twittering? Then he noticed a lizard as it peeked over a rock and darted away and an ant dragging a moth twenty times its size, maneuvering the mass around rocky obstacles.

Vonlai's left ear—the one embedded in dirt—tingled with a blunt pain. Now he had a reason to move. He lifted his head off the ground and rolled it to the other side.

Leaves and gravel plastered the side of his face. He didn't bother to adjust the rest of his body. His heartbeat felt stronger with his chest against the ground, and it reminded him he wasn't dead.

His eyes traveled across the ground like a snake's. He'd have no trouble following Dalah if he could slither along unnoticed.

Something just out of reach caught Vonlai's eye. It was a stick—a perfect Y-shaped branch, thick and straight, exactly suited for making a slingshot. Without a thought to Meh's warning that a slingshot would only bring him more trouble, he belly-crawled to the stick and snatched it right away.

He sat up and scratched at the drying blood on his right cheek. From the left side of his face, he peeled off leaves and plucked out pebbles. When he stood to brush off his knees, Vonlai realized he'd lost a flip-flop.

He tucked the stick into his pants at the waist and retraced his steps up the hill. He spotted his sandal wedged between the ground and the jutting rock that had sent him sailing, but the strap was torn. Pah would scold him, but he could make him a new pair by tracing his feet on old tires and cutting them up for soles. He'd use inner tube for the straps, and Vonlai could use a leftover strip to make a sling for his stick.

He headed toward a shallow creek bed to collect stones.

He needed just the right shape and size, smooth and round, but not too big. The leaves fluttering overhead sounded like running water, but monsoon season was light, so the creek was only a mud pit waiting to be washed alive again.

Vonlai heard a whistle he couldn't place. He stopped to listen. It was certainly no bird he'd ever heard. He cocked his head to the side. It wasn't coming from the treetops or the shrubby undergrowth. It was down near the creek bed.

Vonlai made his way closer, and there lying on his back, with bare feet propped on a rock and a hand behind his head as a pillow, a man smoked a cigarette. Vonlai thought he acted more like a tourist on a white sand beach than a penniless refugee.

Between whistles, the man blew smoke rings at the sky. He made one long oval that wafted away like a lazy ghost. Then he blew five or six tight rings that trailed after each other like elephants in line, trunks to tails.

Three men suddenly came out from the trees on the opposite side of the creek. Vonlai squatted behind a clump of bamboo. He recognized them from his barracks. One man had no arm below his left elbow, just a lumpy pink stump that still wiggled as it searched for a hand to operate. The other two men had daughters about Dalah's age. These men had fought on the front lines in the war and knew how to walk soundlessly over stones and sticks like a feather glides across skin.

"Miserable Brother," one man said as he hovered over the cigarette smoker.

The man choked on his own breath and sat up fast. His eyes darted back and forth at the men who surrounded him, and he fell back on his hands, scrambling like a crab. The circle tightened around him.

"You shamed my daughter—my family—you snake! Was our suffering in this place not enough?"

"Get up, you homeless dog," another said. "You're going to pay."

"I didn't do it! I swear it wasn't—"

Wham! The three men were on him in a flash. Punching. Stomping. Kicking the man without another word spoken. The cigarette went flying and rolled next to a rock.

Vonlai winced as the man's face got bloodied. Between the blows, the man shrieked for mercy.

It only made things worse. "Mercy? You want mercy, you pig? How did you answer my daughter when she begged for the same thing?"

Vonlai was shaking. His legs were limp. He had to get out of there. He crawled away from his hiding place, sweating but cold, and stood like a toddler unsure of his steps. Putting one foot forward, then the other, Vonlai tore up the hill.

The sound of fists pounding flesh and feet cracking bones trailed after him. Then suddenly, nothing. The shrieking and the mashing and the kicking stopped.

Vonlai winced as the silence sliced into him. Had the man passed out? Or had he taken his final breath?

He pictured the abandoned cigarette dying in the dirt, barely able to send a wisp of smoke into the sky. He remembered the whimpering he'd heard behind the soccer field. And Vonlai remembered Meh's command to never leave Dalah alone.

Tell your sister I miss her.

Vonlai's pulse bashed around inside his skull, and he dropped to his knees to scoop up as many slingshot stones as would fit in his pockets. His feet pounded the trail as he raced out of the grove to find his sister.

With no sense of how much time he'd lost, Vonlai blasted through camp. He checked the soccer field. The group of girls was gone, and so was Dalah. Maybe she'd gone to the water station with Meh, but no, the sun seemed too high to be four o'clock already. It wouldn't even be open yet.

Vonlai stopped to catch his breath. Dalah could be anywhere. He couldn't go home until he found her. He rounded the medical building to check their favorite spot on the hill. He checked the front entrance of Na Pho to see if she was watching the merchants hawk their wares.

Then he saw the trucks. The staples trucks had come, delivering soap, fish sauce, sugar. It was almost as good as the meat trucks. But the unloading was done, and people were headed back home. Maybe Dalah was eager to wash herself with a brand-new bar of soap that would lather better than their tiny leftover chip.

He ran past the processing building, past the soccer field, past the latrines, and cut through alleys to get to his room.

Bam! Vonlai smacked straight into his mother, sending a pot full of uncooked rice into the air. "Curse you, careless boy. Look what you've done!"

"Where's Dalah?" Vonlai tried to keep his voice steady.

"Can't you see your dinner in the dirt? If you want anything in your belly tonight, you'll pluck every grain of rice off that ground. Hear me?"

"Where's Dalah, Meh?"

"Get busy, boy!" Vonlai's mother threw the empty pot at his feet and stormed off to the cooking pits.

But where's Dalah? Vonlai asked himself, his stomach quaking. He spit out a mouthful of vomit. "Dalah! Dalah!"

He wanted to run after his mother to tell her he was sorry, sorry that he shirked his responsibility, sorry that he left his sister alone, sorry that he was a miserable son who couldn't even handle one simple task.

"Vonlai." The voice came from the side of the building.

"Right here, Vonlai." Dalah called out from the tiny garden in back of the living quarters. She carried a wimpy bundle of cilantro, plucked early to end its misery at growing on too little water. Her brown face was streaked with red splotches. She'd been crying again.

"I'm right here, Little Brother. If you had as much flesh on your bones as you have speed in your feet, you'd have knocked Meh clean back to Laos! Now what's going on? Oh! What happened to your face?"

Vonlai tried to catch his breath. Dalah's voice was so much softer than earlier in the day—an almost defeated tone. But he couldn't tell her what he'd seen at the creek. Whether the man was dead or not, the guards would come around asking questions. Telling Dalah would only pass the burden of secrecy to her, and he'd done enough for the day.

"I couldn't find you," Vonlai said. "I climbed a tree to get a better look and lost my footing."

"Well, you look as if an evil spirit has hold of your soul. And I'm to blame." Dalah's face showed a hint of a smile, even though it was forced, but she was trying. "Now let's get this rice picked up, then I'll clean that cut for you."

Vonlai nearly buckled at Dalah's offer. He wanted to tear out his hair to escape from the seesaw of emotions that dropped his stomach. He wanted to cry for the girl who was shamed. For his mother whose face always looked flat. For his father who tried to see past

157

his family's desperation. For the brilliance of his friend Kavin, and the world that might never benefit from it. For Colonel who breathed pain every day and relived the horror of captivity every night. And for Dalah. Vonlai wanted to cry for his sister who was safe and smiling and trying to help him, instead of running around with girls whose futures were bound to be grim.

Vonlai and Dalah crouched on the ground. They picked up one grain of rice at a time and tossed them into the cook pot.

Pah would be back soon with firewood, and they would all sit outside on their tattered mat, as they did every night, sharing their meager meal and trying not to forget their dreams.

Chapter
22

Vonlai woke to the sound of a soft rain pattering the roof. A breeze swept in through their open door, and Vonlai saw Dalah standing in the rain. Her face was tilted skyward as she let the water wash over her.

Vonlai crept out of bed, careful not to disturb Pah and Meh. He stood next to Dalah. Without moving, she asked, "What will become of me, Little Brother? What will become of us?"

Vonlai wanted to have an answer, something wise that could comfort Dalah, but he gave the only answer he could. "I don't know."

"Walk me to Kavin's?"

"Now? It's early still."

"We can take the long way around."

"Let me get something first."

Back inside, Pah still snored, but Meh was sitting on

the edge of the bed. She rubbed her whole face in one slow sweep, starting from her chin and moving up through her hair as if to wipe herself clean.

"Dalah and I are going out."

Meh yawned, nodded, and waved him away. Vonlai grabbed his carving knife and the Y-shaped stick he'd found near the creek bed.

Silently, he and Dalah walked through camp. Rain dripped off the roofs and fell into collection bins positioned on the ground. As the sky dried out, a slice of light broke over the horizon and mist rose from the ground to quench the sun's thirst.

"Where are your shoes?" Dalah asked.

"Busted them."

"Wouldn't do you much good today, anyway." Dalah stepped out of her shoes, picked them up, and flung off sticky globs of mud. "I'd keep walking through this muck all day if it would get us somewhere."

Vonlai took care to find the deepest puddles, kneading his toes into the ground. "I think it feels good. Try it."

Dalah turned to look at Vonlai. "How do you keep your spirits up in this place?"

"I don't do it on purpose."

Dalah laughed and joined Vonlai in the puddle. "It's okay. It's a good thing, really. I just don't know how you do it."

Vonlai shrugged as they started off again, socks of mud covering their ankles. They rounded the corner to Kavin's barracks. He was rearranging clothes on the line.

"I'm busting out of this place," Dalah said. "Want to come?"

"Let me grab my hacksaw. And the keys to the getaway car." Kavin packed a couple bottles of water in a rucksack and followed Dalah. Vonlai stood there, wondering if he should bother Colonel this early or go back home to see what Pah and Meh needed him to do.

Dalah turned around and stared at him, her hands on her hips. "Aren't you coming?"

"You want me to come with you?"

"Get your muddy behind over here," she said.

Vonlai ran to catch up, but he slipped in the mud and landed with limbs splayed out like a newborn buffalo. Kavin laughed and came back to help. "You look like a chocolate-covered chopstick."

"A bleeding, chocolate-covered chopstick." Vonlai lifted his shirt to look at his stomach. The slingshot stick he'd carried in the waist of his pants had gouged him when he fell.

"Uh-oh," Kavin said. "You're up to no good with that thing. See? Blood has been spilled already."

Vonlai dabbed his cut with the last speck of shirt that was mud-free. "Got any rubber?"

"You know I do." Kavin ran back to his barracks, then returned to Dalah and Vonlai, a wide smile on his face. They walked to the far edge of camp, where a small hill was just enough to disappear behind if you lay on the ground. The slant of the earth had allowed the water to run off quickly, and the ground was not too muddy.

Vonlai rested on his back, one leg crossed over the other knee, scraping at the dried mud on his ankles. He watched patches of blue take over the sky, then pulled out his stick and knife to begin smoothing the knots off the handle. He gripped the stick in his left hand to test where his knuckles would go, and he carved out subtle indents to craft a better hold.

"Whoa," Kavin said. "You trying to show me up?"

Dalah had her head on Kavin's stomach. She rolled over to see. "Maybe you can catch us dinner with that thing."

Vonlai nodded, never taking his eyes off his work. "Yeah. Maybe."

Kavin reached in his rucksack to grab the scraps of inner tube. "You're not going to hurt a mouse without a sling. Hand it over."

Kavin measured a strip of rubber against Vonlai's arm. He cut the ends, tied them on the stick, and tested the tension. After adjusting the knot on one prong, he handed it to Vonlai. "There you go, Master Turkey Killer."

"What?" Vonlai said. "Did I tell you that story?"

Vonlai felt the sting of shame on his cheeks, as if he'd disappointed his mother only yesterday.

Kavin warbled like a dying turkey. "Your sister did."

Dalah laughed. "I've never seen you dance so fast as when you dodged Meh's switch that day."

"Oh yeah?" Vonlai said, shaking away the memory, not only of the shame, but of his friend Khom, whose laugh was lost to him. "Predators will be dodging me when they see my skill." Vonlai picked up a rock, positioned it in his sling, and drew his arm back. "Third tree over from that barrel. Tip of the dead branch hanging down."

Vonlai let the sling loose, and the rock flew hard but wide. It landed in a shrub with a very unconvincing rustle.

Dalah and Kavin clapped, followed by a round of gobbles. "Maybe we should leave you alone to practice," Kavin said. He hooked his arm in Dalah's as they walked farther down the hill and disappeared behind the bamboo.

Vonlai picked up another rock, rolled it in his palm, and fired away.

Chapter
23

"Where you been, boy?" Colonel asked as Vonlai sat next to him by the soccer field.

"Been working on something." Vonlai handed him the slingshot.

Colonel turned it over in his hands, looking at it from all angles. Then he closed his eyes and ran his fingers gently along the handle, up the prongs, over the ends. He handed it back to Vonlai. "Couldn't have done better myself."

"You shouldn't lie," Vonlai said, knocking a shoulder into Colonel. "You might come back as a snake."

"Good. I'll eat all the rats in the world."

Vonlai picked up one of Colonel's carvings. "When do you suppose we'll get our interviews?"

"Why don't you carve me a crystal ball and I'll have a look," Colonel said.

"I don't think you could see very clearly in a ball made of wood."

"Your time will come."

A soccer ball rolled off the field to Vonlai. He stood to drop-kick it back into the game and sat down again. "Everybody says that."

"Will it do you any good to believe otherwise?"

"I guess not. What about you? Do you believe your time will come?"

"An old man like me fills his brain with memories, not dreams."

Vonlai examined the tigers and crocodiles Colonel had started. "If I could learn to carve like you, Uncle, maybe I could sell figurines to the merchants outside the gates. I want to learn English, not because I'm going anywhere, but I could curse at the guards and they'd never know. There's a man in Building Seven I could pay to teach me."

Colonel threw down his knife. He grabbed Vonlai's face and held it in his hands. "Have I shown myself to be an incompetent teacher?"

Vonlai startled at Colonel's sudden passion. "No. No. But you've already taught me so much. I didn't want to be greedy."

"So you would choose to be stupid instead and waste your money?" Colonel's eyes were glossy, and he released his hold on Vonlai.

"I didn't think it'd be a waste. I'm sorry."

Colonel picked up his knife again. "You *can* get good enough to sell figurines. I have no doubt. But I'll teach you English because you do have a future, so keep your money for that, son."

Vonlai lay awake that night planning his future. He didn't know where he'd end up in the world, but he would try to prepare. Colonel had faith in his talents. Vonlai could earn a little money to stash away, or use to buy a soda or small bag of sticky rice now and then, and still learn English from Colonel for no fee. He'd already begun to forget Miss Chada's lessons, but with Colonel's help, it wouldn't be too late.

Dalah stirred and sat up. Vonlai pretended to be asleep as she crawled off the bed. He went back to his dreams.

Maybe he'd try carving an elephant first like the one Colonel had given him. It was a bulky animal that might prove easier than a crocodile, whose hide would need to appear rough, or a tiger with its long tail. And with the money he'd earn, Meh would welcome a little extra something to cook. That was the one time she always seemed to perk up. Back in Laos, she and Dalah used to spend half the afternoon rolling out and slicing noodles for soup.

Where *was* Dalah? Vonlai wondered. She should be back from the latrines by now. Vonlai shot up and pulled on a pair of pants. The stones he'd collected from the creek bed rattled in his pocket and he clamped a hand over them.

He rushed into the night to the block of latrines and waited. He listened at the door that was closest to their barracks. "Dalah?" he whispered. Vonlai continued down the row. "Dalah?"

Finally he heard a noise, but it came from behind him, away from the latrines. It was a muffled cry. A struggle of wills. And a command. "Shut up!"

The scuffling moved farther away. Vonlai raced up the hill. A man stifled his own cry of pain, and Vonlai heard a vigorous smack. "Don't bite me again, you little priss!"

The voices trailed off—the unmistakable bark of Tiger Tong and the familiar cry of Dalah.

Vonlai strained his eyes and barely made out two struggling shadows across the field. They moved into the brush. Vonlai reached into his pocket for a stone, but he had no sling. He'd left it hidden behind their room so Meh wouldn't find it.

Vonlai flew to the barracks. He slid feetfirst near the nook where he'd hidden his slingshot and grappled in the dark. He grabbed it and tore back up the hill, but his racing feet were too loud. His breath raged like a blowtorch. He was going to give himself away. Vonlai suddenly remembered his father's words the very night they left Laos.

Walk like a tiger hunting a meal, Pah had said.

Vonlai streamlined his lumbering pace. He imagined

himself racing behind a ball carrier whose overconfidence at a clear goal was his downfall. Vonlai was fast, sneaky, and deathly quiet. Players claimed he could come out of nowhere, same as a lost spirit wandering into the wrong house.

The noise from the brush was plenty loud. Tiger Tong was anything but cautious. Vonlai tracked him easily.

"You fight this hard with that boyfriend of yours?" Tong said through gritted teeth.

"You're scum," Dalah managed, then shrieked with pain at some unseen reprimand.

Vonlai crouched and crept along the brush, but he couldn't see a thing.

The sound of a thud nearly made him vomit. A fist in flesh. He heard a body fall. His sister's body, retching, desperate for air.

Where were they, exactly? It was pitch-dark in the shrub.

"I gave you a chance," Tong said.

Vonlai whispered to himself. "Keep talking, Tong. Keep talking." He slipped his hand in his pocket for a stone and positioned it in the rubber.

Vonlai heard clothing tear.

He had to take a shot. He raised his sling, but his hands were shaking.

Master Turkey Killer.

You missed your target.

Vonlai took a breath and let it out slowly.

You'll only get in more trouble with that thing.

Your boy killed my livestock.

Vonlai closed his eyes, like Colonel did to inspect a carving, and he listened.

Dalah whimpered.

"Oh, shut up," Tong said.

Vonlai adjusted his position. *Keep talking, you snake.*

"Jun liked it, so relax."

Vonlai held his breath and let it fly. A sound shot out, like a pestle striking an empty mortar. Vonlai opened his eyes, but he couldn't see if he hit his target—or his sister.

Then a scream. "Get off me! Get off me!" He heard a body roll into the brush. Dalah must have pushed Tong off her. She ran out past the shrub and Vonlai made out her shadow. She'd gotten away. He'd hit his target and Dalah had gotten away.

In the brush, he heard Tong groan and mumble. Vonlai had to get out of there. He tore after Dalah. She checked behind her as she ran and screamed. "No! Get away from me."

"It's me, Dalah," Vonlai tried to whisper as they ran.

"No! Get away!"

Tong was going to hear them. Vonlai had no choice. He had to tackle her. He caught up to Dalah, grabbed her waist, and as they fell, he twisted his body underneath hers to break her fall. Her fists rained down on his head. "No! No! No!"

"It's me, Sister. It's Vonlai."

But she writhed out of his hold and tried to scamper away, still screaming.

"Dalah, it's Vonlai! Tong will hear us. Please."

"What? Vonlai?" She grabbed his ears to hold his face still and tried to see him in the dark. "It's you," she said, and clasped her arms around his neck, sobbing into his chest. "Thank you, Brother. Thank you. Thank you. Thank you."

"We need to move away from here. Tong was starting to stir."

"I can't go home yet."

"He didn't—"

"No," Dalah said between heavy breaths. "You got there in time. How did you know?"

"Let's move out of here. It's near morning. We can sit by the fire pit until you're ready to go back inside. He won't touch us there."

Vonlai helped Dalah up and together they ran, his arm hooked through hers, pulling her along.

Chapter
24

Before the sun even rose, the thick morning air foretold a day of punishing heat. Dalah and Vonlai sat under a lightening sky and sipped water.

"Look at my legs," Dalah said to Vonlai, scraping at dried blood. "They're all scratched up. Meh will notice."

"Notice? You mean you're not going to tell her?"

"No." She wiped tears off her cheeks.

"But you have to. She should know."

"So she can fret even more? Withdraw into herself deeper? She doesn't need that. Besides, she'd never let me out of sight again, even with you tailing me, and I'll never see—oh, never mind." Dalah stood up to go inside. She tried to straighten her skirt, but the tear made that impossible.

Vonlai knew his sister was worried she wouldn't get to see Kavin again. And that would hurt him as much as her.

Vonlai didn't want to see his friend—or his family—suffer anymore.

"I'll wear a long sarong till my cuts heal. Don't tell Meh or Pah. Please?"

Vonlai nodded. "Better hurry up. I hear them stirring."

Dalah bent down to hug him and spoke softly in his ear. "Thank you. You weren't a turkey killer for nothing, Brother."

Meh had Vonlai and Dalah doing morning chores, cleaning pots, wiping the dust off the walls in their room. Vonlai had never seen Dalah scrub harder at anything. Pah and three other men dragged part of a dead tree to the open area in front of the barracks. They took turns with the ax, hacking it into stool-size seats for gatherings around the fire pits.

Meh handed Dalah a pile of clothes. "These need soaking." She pulled Dalah's hair away from her face. "What's happened to your eye?"

Dalah's hand shot up to cover it. "What?"

"It's bruised."

Vonlai watched her. He hadn't seen the bruise earlier—it must have showed up gradually as the hours passed.

"Oh, that," Dalah said. "Last night, I smacked right into a latrine door that some fool left open."

"Be more careful next time," Meh said. "It's dangerous walking in the dark."

Vonlai saw Dalah's chin start to quiver, but Meh moved on to the next chore. Dalah took a deep breath and went back to her clothes.

"When we're done, let's go see Kavin," Vonlai said. "Drag his lazy rear out of bed."

Dalah smiled at the thought and nodded. Then she locked her eyes on Vonlai. "Don't tell him, Vonlai. Please. He'll be spitting mad and go off and do something to get himself in trouble."

"Are you going to tell anyone about this? Ever?" Vonlai asked.

"Jun never did. Must be a good reason to keep quiet."

At Kavin's door, his father stopped Vonlai and Dalah. "He's not well today. Can't take any visitors."

"Pah?" Kavin called. His voice was weak. His illness must have come on quick, Vonlai thought. "Let them in."

Kavin's father stepped aside. "Maybe some company will do him good. Don't worry. What he's got isn't contagious."

Vonlai followed Dalah into the room, but she screamed and jumped back. "You're hurt!" Dalah said. She fell to her knees at his bedside, hesitated, then gently touched his head. He lay on his side and was bloodied from head to toe. A bruise on his back in the shape of a boot was starting to show.

"Who did this to you?" Vonlai asked.

"Guards. Came knocking this morning." Kavin paused to focus on breathing. "Said we were approved for interviews. Some glitch in paperwork. Pah was gone so I went. Then bam."

"They lied about your interview?" Dalah said. "What did they have against you?"

Kavin worked up the wind to keep talking. "Payback. For putting Tong's eye out."

"Tong's eye is out?" Vonlai asked, giving Dalah a look. "Are you sure?"

"They said so. But I didn't do it."

Dalah stood up and paced the room. "Vonlai, what should we do?"

"We have to report him. He can't get away with this."

Kavin struggled to adjust his position. He winced and moaned.

Dalah rushed to help him. "You shouldn't move. Sit still."

Kavin turned his head to look at Dalah with the eye that had the least swelling. "You're hurt, too." He reached up to touch the bruise on her face.

"I fell."

"You're lying. He hurt you, didn't he?" Kavin gritted

his teeth as he propped himself up on one elbow. "You tell me what happened."

Dalah burst into tears and covered her face. "Nothing happened. Nothing. Because Vonlai came. He came in time with his slingshot."

Kavin put a hand on Dalah's back and looked at Vonlai. "Little Brother?"

"We have to report him," Vonlai said, staring at the walls. "Tong won't leave girls alone until we report him."

"Are you crazy?" Kavin said. "He'll figure out it was you who took out his eye and he'll do the same to you as he did to me. Or worse."

"I don't care."

Kavin lunged forward and grabbed Vonlai's elbow, pulling him to the ground despite his own pain. "You listen to me! As it stands now, he thinks the person who took half his vision has paid his due. Now leave it be. But we can't let Dalah out of our sight."

"Then I'm nothing but a chicken!" Vonlai said. "Look what he's done to you both. I'm letting him win."

"He didn't win," Dalah said, rocking gently with her knees pulled into her chest. "He didn't."

"Colonel will know what to do," Vonlai said. "There's nothing I can't talk to him about."

"Don't you get it, Little Brother?" Vonlai heard a shift in Kavin's voice. He saw the pleading in his eyes. "Let

Tong think the right person has paid. Let me carry your secret for the rest of my life, so at least I have a reason to wake up each day in this place. Besides, that old man doesn't deserve to hear any more about the evil people are willing to inflict on each other. Please. Time will pass more smoothly if I can at least know my silence serves to keep you safe."

Vonlai refused to let any tears fall in front of his friend, even though a well of sorrow boiled behind his eyes. He looked at Dalah, and when her face showed no objection, Vonlai nodded his agreement.

Exhausted, Kavin fell back on the bed and laid his forearm across his eyes. And Vonlai and Dalah stayed near him in the days ahead, holding the secret between them, as Kavin fell in and out of sleep, the pain on his flesh making itself known with each labored breath.

Chapter
25

January 1986

Monsoon season had come and gone four times since Vonlai entered Na Pho. Jun had been gone more than three years now. Her letters from America had arrived a few months after she left. Some even included a ten-dollar bill, and the merchants outside the gates clamored to give the best deals to those with American money. Jun included photographs, too. Pictures of herself standing in front of her high school holding armloads of books. One with her being swallowed by a puffy coat with a fur-trimmed hood, leaning against a plowed pile of snow two-people tall. Another of her waving from a parking lot with a sports stadium behind her—*Home of the Minnesota Vikings*.

After that first letter had come, Dalah read it over and

over, day after day, before finally letting Vonlai take it to show Kavin.

"So what?" Kavin had said, barely pausing to read a few words.

"What do you mean so what? It'll happen for us. This is proof."

Kavin handed it back. "The letters will stop. Give it six months. Maybe a year—tops."

"But Jun was Dalah's best friend," Vonlai insisted.

"Like I said . . . so what? Jun has a new best friend now. Guarantee it. Nobody who gets out of this place wants to remember what they left behind."

Vonlai had never told Kavin what Tiger Tong had said he did to Jun, but somehow Vonlai thought he probably knew. Kavin knew too much about Na Pho and the people who languished here, and putting the ugliness into words wouldn't make it go away. Kavin grabbed his soccer ball and headed to the field. He didn't ask Vonlai to join him.

Vonlai had fetched his carving knife from home and gone to sit in the shady spot outside the school. Colonel was in bed fighting a cough, and Vonlai didn't like to carve alone. At least outside the school, Vonlai could still hear the lessons taught by Miss Chada's replacement. The teachers' faces changed too often, though, for him to bother knowing them. Besides, he wasn't a student anymore.

Time had proved Kavin right. The letters came five months in a row. Then two months would pass before another came. Then three months, and like water dripping off hanged laundry, the letters stopped. After nearly a year with nothing, Dalah stopped racing to meet the mail truck.

Vonlai always returned to his wood carving. After more than three years working next to Colonel, Vonlai had honed his ability to turn scraps of wood into works of art. And he incorporated his first love, architecture, into his craft. He carved villages and temples in addition to animals, and the Thai merchants regularly paid him for his work, transporting them to tourist areas where Westerners were eager to buy a keepsake of their trip to tropical paradise. Vonlai bought better cuts of wood, a few carving tools, and a little extra food to keep Meh busy cooking.

New faces showed up every month—eleven years after the war ended—even though fewer and fewer buses came to transport them out, but questioning his fate was a waste of time. It was a method of survival he'd learned from Colonel, who always possessed a certain calm by refusing to struggle against destiny.

Vonlai could barely comprehend that he was sixteen years old now, a veteran refugee who involved the new-comers on the soccer field as Kavin had done for him four years ago. Vonlai carved numbers to hook on a pegboard so the smallest kids could play scorekeeper. Even a new boy, Linh, who'd lost half a leg on a land mine, could play. His spirit was roused when he hobbled downfield with his crutch, and Vonlai was glad the boy hadn't thought to ask him how long he'd been at Na Pho.

If Kavin didn't show up to play by midmorning, Vonlai went to fetch him from bed. He visited his barracks nearly every day to rouse him.

"Kavin, you sloth," Vonlai hollered from outside. He pushed a half-built wheelbarrow out of the way. Wheelbarrows had become Kavin's specialty, and he built them for refugees who had money to pay so he could buy more materials to build toys for those who didn't. Vonlai went in and stood at his bedside. "The guys say Linh is faster than you even with his one leg."

"I don't doubt it," Kavin mumbled, kicking at the space where Vonlai stood.

Vonlai poured water on a rag. "Get up, Grandpa," he said as he threw the towel on Kavin's head.

"You assface!" Kavin shot straight up and a wave of stale alcohol wafted to Vonlai. "My head still hurts, Skeleton Boy."

"Why are you complaining? Your head hurts every morning, but you still drink every night. Now come run that poison out of your blood so you can see straight."

"I don't want to see straight," Kavin said, but he pushed himself off the bed, anyway. He threw the sopping towel back at Vonlai as they made their way out the door to pass the morning hours chasing balls in the dirt.

Chapter
26

March 1986

It was an unusually cool evening, especially for the dry season, during Vonlai's fourth year in Na Pho when the news came. It spread through camp like water from a cracked levee, soaking every barracks with sorrow. Colonel had passed in his sleep.

Vonlai sat balled up on the bed as Pah told him the news. He curled himself around the tiny elephant Colonel had carved for him so many years ago. He pressed his thumb into the ragged edge where a tusk had broken off, but even that had dulled over time, and it wasn't sharp enough to cut him to divert the pain in his heart.

Vonlai woke the next morning, a blanket of grief gripping his skin.

"Pah and I are going to help dress the body," Meh said,

duty and obligation driving her. "Kavin's waiting for you outside. And Dalah's here, too."

Vonlai stood up. The wooden elephant fell to the ground. Vonlai rubbed the indent on his stomach where he'd lain curved around the carving all night. Outside, he sat on the mat by the cook fire. Dalah and Kavin shared a tree stump. Vonlai couldn't do anything but stare at their feet.

"His suffering is over now, Little Brother," Dalah said.

"Was it worth it for him to come here?" Vonlai asked, raking his fingers over the ground. "He wanted a better life and instead he breathes his last breath in this dusty dungeon."

"You gave him a better life," Kavin said. "You were his friend."

"He humored me, that's all," Vonlai said. "He didn't have the heart to tell a bothersome kid to go away."

Vonlai grabbed his carving knife. "Kavin, will you stay with Dalah? I'm taking off for awhile."

Kavin nodded, and as Vonlai walked past them, Dalah put her head on Kavin's shoulder. Kavin wrapped his arm around her waist, and they leaned into each other.

Under the mango tree, Vonlai ran his hand along the bark in the exact spot where Colonel always sat, then slumped against the trunk. Kids still ran on the soccer field, oblivious to the fact that the universe had just shifted. Vonlai didn't know when the Colonel was born, or even what his real name was, but this was the spot they shared for nearly four years, the spot where Colonel had fed Vonlai's dreams. Vonlai wouldn't let anyone forget that Colonel had lived and breathed and tried to thrive in this place. He remembered a phrase Colonel had told him about America. *Home of the Brave.*

Vonlai turned toward the tree, dug the knife into the bark, and carved those words deep into the wood.

The three days of mourning passed. A monk from a Thai village was on his way to perform the funeral service.

Vonlai picked up the lopsided soccer ball he'd carved with Colonel for his first project. He squeezed it in his fist and walked with Pah, Meh, and Dalah to Colonel's barracks. Colonel lay on his bed, dressed in the finest silk formal wear his neighbors could afford. Vonlai lit a stick of incense at his shrine and prayed for a swift passage into his next life.

"It's time," Vonlai's mother said.

Men who served under Colonel in the Royal Lao Army lifted his body into the casket. Vonlai supported a corner of the wooden box as they carried it past the temple to the outskirts of camp. They laid it atop a pile of logs for cremation.

The roaring fire scorched Vonlai's cheeks. He lifted his head to watch the blaze. Through the heat, the casket wavered as if the air itself was melting.

Vonlai stood his ground until there was nothing but ashes and the glow of embers.

Bless you, Colonel, Vonlai thought. You finally found your way out of this place.

And then the fear exploded inside Vonlai. Was his family doomed to get out the same way? A couple of months in Na Pho had turned into four years, and what was to stop four years from turning into a lifetime?

Vonlai felt a weight on his arm, a hand squeezing his shoulder. He turned to see Pah standing next to him, the orange glow of Colonel's fading funeral pyre reflected in his eyes. Pah's face harbored that confident look he'd worn ever since they came to Na Pho, and it was deep and peaceful. Maybe because Colonel was at peace now, no longer suffering from his mangled ankle and his shredded heart.

Vonlai bent his head down to press his face against Pah's shoulder, and the tears flowed. Vonlai tried to gulp air between sobs. The pain cut as deep as the night he nearly drowned in the Mekong, and Vonlai clung to Pah's neck the same way he did when the river had tried to swallow him.

On that night back in 1982, Vonlai held tight to the idea that life would get better soon. They would go to America. Pah would work again. Meh would have a house and a garden to tend. He and Dalah would make friends and go to the best schools in the world. They could build a new life, and everything would be okay again—someday.

But someday never came for Colonel. It hadn't come for Kavin. And it might never come for him. Vonlai wondered if there would be anybody to cry for him at his own funeral after he sucked in his final breath of Na Pho air.

Meh and Dalah hooked their arms through Vonlai's elbows and started back home. Frogs bellowed their chorus in the dusk, and the birds began their twilight twittering as if the whole world had been waiting for their songs.

Halfway home, as the ruby horizon painted its goodnight wishes across the sky, Pah cleared his throat. "I have news. Now is as good a time as any to share it. We are scheduled for interviews tomorrow."

The words floated away in the night air, and Vonlai repeated them in his head. *We are scheduled for interviews tomorrow.*

Vonlai's face was still wet from tears, but he jumped in the air. Dalah shrieked like a four-year-old on her first carousel ride. A waft of funeral smoke filled Vonlai's lungs, and he suddenly remembered that only a moment ago, his heart had been gushing grief. The swing of emotion dropped Vonlai to his knees, and just when he thought he'd burned up all his tears, the stream came again.

"Oh, why couldn't Colonel have lived a few more days?" Vonlai said. "Just a few days—so he could hear my news."

"Vonlai," Meh said, cradling his head. "Maybe it's better this way. Colonel's heart would have broken all over again had you left him here alone."

"But he should've gotten out, too," Vonlai said. "He was an officer. Even with no documents, anybody would know him—they could prove who he was. Why didn't anybody vouch for him? Why?"

"Colonel's heart was heavy, child," Meh said. "Vonlai, please understand. He could have had his interviews years ago if he'd wanted."

Vonlai looked up from his place where he crouched in the dirt. "What are you talking about, Meh? Why was he still in here then?"

"After he met you," Pah said, "he felt like he had a family again. He didn't want to leave by himself to start over in a new place with no one to love."

Vonlai grabbed his own hair with both fists. "I should have seen it. I could have told him he could live with us in America someday, couldn't he?"

"No," Meh said. "It was too late for Colonel. He sold his identity, Vonlai. He sold it to a man whose wife and children got released without him. He gave another man a chance to get his family back. And in this camp, Colonel had you, Vonlai. You were a son to him after he lost his own all those years ago."

Vonlai turned to the funeral site and squeezed the little carved soccer ball in his hand. It all made sense now. Colonel always spoke as if he knew he would never leave Na Pho, saying his fate was set. He never spoke of his own future. He never spoke of his own dreams, only Vonlai's. "When you get to America," Colonel had said, "send me a letter. When you graduate from high school, send me a picture. And when you build your first skyscraper, stand at the very top and wave to me from across the world."

Vonlai wanted to go back in time, even if it meant having to wait all over again for interviews, just so he could have another day with Colonel. He wanted to sit next to him again under the mango tree, and prove there was more to the spirit of Vonlai Sirivong than a selfish, uncaring pest who could see only his own problems, dream only of his own future.

Vonlai yearned to throw his carving into the smoldering fire pit, to burn the evidence of Colonel's unappreciated devotion, but he couldn't do it. Vonlai's faith had bled into that ball. Colonel's teaching had saved him from despair—made him believe in his own worth. That lopsided ball would always remind him to never give up. To find victory in the most unexpected places. To build himself up, even when the world had forgotten him.

As Vonlai rolled the little ball between his hands, he watched the tendrils of smoke disappear into the sky and imagined himself waving to Colonel from the top of a building that kissed the clouds.

Chapter
27

Pah completed a set of documents and joined Meh, Dalah, and Vonlai on the bench in front of the panel of Joint Volunteer Agency men waiting to interview them. A framed picture of the Thai king and queen hung high on the wall, and the pair watched Vonlai from their mounted position of reverence above all the other framed documents and maps.

"So this is your family, Boune?" a representative asked.

"Yes, sir," Pah said. "My wife, Davone, and my two children."

"Can you tell us about your background? What you did in Laos?"

Vonlai sat, back straight, on the wooden bench. He focused on a fan blowing in the corner, but it barely nudged the thick air.

The officials thumbed through their papers, and Vonlai

silently begged. *Please let us out. Please let us out. Please let us out.* Between prayers to his ancestors and pleas to Buddha, Vonlai caught only bits of his father's answers.

"... architectural apprenticeship in Paris ... residential home design ... Royal Lao Army ..."

And then a pinch under his arm. Dalah had reached over to jar him from his drifting mind.

"Your name, young man?" A different man from the JVA asked in English, one with gray hair and a thin mustache. He had pale skin and round eyes and wore a pin of an American flag that appeared to be waving in the wind. He looked squarely at Vonlai as the interpreter translated his question.

"I am Vonlai Sirivong, sixteen years old." He was relieved to hear that his voice worked. His throat was raw from the night before, breathing in the smoke from Colonel's cremation.

"Can you tell us about living in Laos? The Pathet Lao? It wasn't so bad now, was it?"

Vonlai's mind panicked as he heard the translation. The question was a trick. He'd heard others talk about it. The interviewers want to make sure you have no hidden loyalty to the Communists. What could he tell them to make them understand?

Vonlai glanced at his parents for guidance, but they both looked straight ahead. Then his blood ran cold, gelling inside his veins as the memory gushed forth.

"*Son, what was it like?*" The man asked again through the interpreter. He adjusted a stack of papers on the desk. "*Can you tell us?*"

"They killed my dog," Vonlai mumbled.

"*Can you speak up, son?*"

The interpreter began to translate, but Vonlai interrupted, speaking partly in English. "*I understand question.* I said they killed my dog."

"*Your dog?*"

Vonlai closed his eyes and reached between his knees to squeeze the bench. "There were three of them. Pathet Lao soldiers not much older than I am now. They sat around a fire, guns at their feet. They said black dogs—solid black like mine—were lucky to eat. I saw them skinning her. I didn't believe them at first. I didn't believe it was my dog, but when I got home, she was gone. They gave my mother a can of gasoline and took my dog."

Meh covered her face. Her shoulders trembled with silent sobs. Vonlai couldn't hold back. Eleven years worth of rancid emotion bubbled out of him, and he wept, spilling the hatred he'd had to swallow in order to survive living among them—the lying Communists. The Pathet Lao soldiers who stole from his family, dragged people away in the night, bullied his father, destroyed his country, and slaughtered his dog.

The men looked up from their note taking. Vonlai filled his lungs with a chalky breath.

"Well, Mr. Vonlai Sirivong. We appreciate your candor," the translator said. "It appears everything is in order. We have granted your family's request for political asylum and approved your relocation to the United States of America. We have located the cousin of Boune Sirivong who has agreed to sponsor your family, and after you have acquired employment, you will be required, over time, to reimburse the government for your plane fare. Vannasak Vongsavanh and his family are waiting for you in Kansas. In nine days, you'll be on your way."

Vonlai sat motionless on the bench. Dalah squeezed his leg as Pah reached around Meh's shoulder to rub his neck. Meh pressed her hands together in the prayer symbol and raised them to the sky.

"Now if you'll proceed outside, we'll finalize these remaining exit documents and get you photographed. Congratulations, Sirivong family. Good luck to you all."

A sultry breeze kicked up and clean white clouds sailed overhead. Onlookers stood watching from a distance, a few coming close to shake Pah's hand. The smiles on their faces did nothing to hide the desolation in their eyes.

The photographer lined up Vonlai's family from oldest to youngest and handed Pah a chalkboard with numbers on it. "Hold that up now, Mr. Sirivong."

Meh's mouth turned up at the corners as Pah held the board firmly in his hands, his shoulders straight. Vonlai could barely keep his feet on the ground for all the energy that raced through his bones. Dalah bumped her shoulder against Vonlai, and the camera snapped their picture.

On the way home, Meh stopped at the Na Pho gate and handed money to Dalah and Vonlai. "Go buy potatoes and coconut milk."

"You think you still remember how to cook dessert?" Pah joked. He bought packs of cigarettes and a bag of hard candy. Vonlai knew they'd have a throng of visitors at their place tonight. He had attended many farewell parties for others who left before them, and the melancholy mood of the well-wishers was lightened a bit with a taste of something sweet and a good smoke.

At home, Linh, the boy with one leg, was there waiting with Kavin. Vonlai could hardly bear to look at him.

"The news is good, friend," Kavin said, holding out his hand to shake Vonlai's.

"Yes, it's very good," Vonlai said, wrapping both his hands around Kavin's. "You'll stay and eat with us tonight, right?"

"Where else would I be?"

Meh sliced the potatoes into bite-sized bits to boil, then soaked them in coconut milk and sugar. Dalah carried out a tray of sliced mango. Kavin's eyes followed her. "Excuse me, Little Brother." He took the tray from her and set it on the mat. He pulled her tight into his arms. Dalah's tears fell freely as she let him hold her.

Around the fire pit, Pasong the beggar sat strumming his guitar, a lantern blazing beside him while his twin toddlers entertained the crowd with a dance. Neighbors milled around to wish Vonlai's family well. They tossed their chicken portions into one giant cook pot. Pah passed cigarettes around to the men but had to snatch them back from kids who sneaked them from his pocket. He tossed candy into the air and sent them scrambling. There was papaya with peppers, Meh's potato dessert, beer, bottles of soda, bowls of Thai noodles, and overhead, there was a sky full of stars shining their light on Vonlai.

On the day of their departure, nothing was left to give away. All the cook pots had been handed off to neighbors. The wheelbarrow Pah built to carry water was gone, as were their water bottles, bedding, baskets, mosquito net, and crates they used to hold their clothes.

Vonlai found newspaper to wrap all the carvings he hadn't sold, and he handed them out to the children, making them promise to share. They shrieked as they unwrapped gifts of snarling tigers, floppy-eared elephants, fierce dragons, and plenty of soccer balls—flawless wooden spheres. But Vonlai carefully rolled the elephant from Colonel into a cloth and tucked it into his waist pouch. When Colonel first held out the carving for Vonlai when he was twelve years old, he'd said it was a guardian for travelers. Vonlai could hardly believe the elephant would finally serve its purpose. And the lopsided ball he'd hung on to all these years went into his right pocket so he could easily reach it to occupy his nervous hands.

The buses sputtered up to the gate. A crowd of onlookers watched as families dragged their bags onto the bus.

"I'm going to write you, Kavin."

Kavin nodded and managed a smile. "I know you will, Little Brother. Now get on that bus before they forget all about you."

Vonlai wasn't going to tell Kavin his time would come. Kavin had heard that enough over the years, and there was talk spreading through camp of forced repatriation, where refugees had to return to the country they'd tried to escape, so Vonlai only spoke the truth. "You've been a good friend, brother."

Kavin squeezed Vonlai's shoulders. "Do something for me then. One last thing."

Vonlai nodded.

"Take care of your sister, would you?"

"You don't have to worry about that. Ever."

Vonlai walked up the stairs, down the aisle, and scooted in next to Dalah. She had her legs pulled into her chest, her head lain across her knees sideways to watch Kavin out the window. He caught her eyes, tapped his heart, and waved good-bye. Dalah kissed her palm and touched the window.

As the engine turned over, riders yelled out to loved ones left behind.

"You'll be next! Stay healthy. We'll pray for you!"

The bus wheels began to roll, creeping along the road. Outside, refugees reached up to touch the hands, one last time, of those who were granted freedom.

Vonlai focused his eyes on Kavin. He had Linh, the one-legged boy, perched on his shoulders, and Noy with his wheelbarrow at his side. Vonlai would never forget. Never.

The tires started to kick up dust. Vonlai waved out the window one last time, then clenched his fists together, digging his fingernails into his palms. He needed his ball. The lopsided, worn, oil-soaked soccer ball he'd bled to create. He reached for it buried inside his pocket, pulled it out, and rolled it in his hands. Without hesitation, Vonlai stuck his head out the window and yelled to Kavin. "Get ready, Grandpa!"

Vonlai pulled his head back in and stuck out his arm. With one swift pitch, he sent the ball sailing through the air. Kavin didn't have to move a single step. He only had to open his palm to catch it, and the ball landed firmly in his hand.

Chapter
28

USA, April 1986

As the plane dipped toward Los Angeles International Airport, so did Vonlai's stomach. It looked as though they'd land in the water, but as the buildings rose to meet them, Vonlai's excitement soared.

"Look at it," Vonlai said. "Look at those buildings. They really do almost touch the clouds. And that tangle of highways. How in the world do they build all that? How do they do it?"

"Move your big head so I can see, you window hog!" Dalah pulled Vonlai's shoulder back. "Wow! There must be a hundred planes down there. Where in the world is everybody going?"

"I can't believe it," Vonlai said. "We get to go to school in America. Look at this city, Dalah. Look what

198

they know how to do."

When the plane landed, the passengers filed out, half of them refugees with connecting flights that would spread them all over the country. Pah had passed around a book to collect addresses. Meh couldn't stop smiling.

In the airport, people stared. The group of refugees, so thin, with skin brown to the bone, stood out among the pasty Americans with their loads of flesh. Rolling, dimpling, beautiful flesh.

"Dalah," Vonlai whispered, "look how rich they all must be to have such fat skin, so healthy. There must be enough food here to feed the whole planet. I can't wait to get that fat."

Pah clutched the vinyl bag with a zippered top. It held the freshly typed UNHCR documents, their most important possession, their proof they had a right to be here. The Lao guide showed them to the next gate.

A group of men, important looking in their suits and briefcases and hurried pace, sidestepped them. Even though the men's faces were different with their sharp noses and light eyes, their expressions mirrored that of the woman on the bank of Thailand who cursed Vonlai's family when they dragged their drenched bodies out of the Mekong.

Vonlai was happy to get back on the connecting plane. He'd barely slept in the two days it took to get from Na Pho to L.A., and now that his eyes had soaked in his first glimpse of America, he could close them and enjoy his dreams.

"Where are all the skyscrapers?" Vonlai rubbed the sleep from his eyes and pressed his face against the window, checking in every direction as the plane descended.

Pah chuckled. "This is Kansas, son. Not Los Angeles."

The runway cut through fields of feathery green plants that swayed—like rice paddies in Laos! No skyscrapers. No highways. No motor scooters jamming the streets or vendors pushing carts of hot noodles like back in Vientiane when Khom rode his handlebars. Only a few flat buildings that looked like fallen dominoes.

Kansas, USA, was a field. Vonlai fell back against the seat. He'd come all the way from the other side of the world to start his life over in a field. Oh, how Khom would laugh to find out his new home looked more like a Lao farm than those glossy magazine pictures they stole peeks at!

In the Kansas City airport, there was no hustle like there'd been in Los Angeles. The airport was clean and quiet, with polished wood floors that reflected the light flowing in the windows.

A family of four stood grinning and waving behind a painted sign that had letters outlined in red, white, and blue. Vonlai read the words out loud in English. *"Welcome, Sirivong Family!"*

At the Vongsavanh house, there was much to adjust to. Pah's cousin, Vannasak, had married a white woman— a *falang*. Her cooking was the worst—its creamy, cheesy, butter-coated casseroles with vegetables so mushy, they fell apart on the fork. He learned the word *dairy* quickly, after it tore through his stomach and became his new enemy.

Dalah whispered to Vonlai as they lay in sleeping bags in the basement, their stomachs roiling. "We might die from lack of edible food much quicker here than in Na Pho!"

And there were the American accents of Vannasak's wife, Joyce, and their two teenaged children, Virginia and Dakota. The English Vonlai learned from Miss Chada and Colonel sounded nothing like what the Vongsavanh family spoke. Virginia and Dakota understood the Lao language, but they didn't speak it. Vonlai did a lot of nodding and smiling and cartoon watching to figure out the words. He braved the language that evening by talking with Dakota in English.

"Need shower from long trip airplane. I'm stink."

Dakota nearly choked on a fire-colored cracker called a Dorito. *"Man, you're not stink. You're stinky."*

"Yes, I'm stink," Vonlai insisted.

Dakota laughed all the way down the hall as he showed Vonlai the shower. *"Vonlai, seriously, try not to talk about your*

B.O.—*I mean body odor, in public. Just trust me on this one. Okay, Stink?"*

But the language was only one difficulty. There was the problem with school. A man from the Lao community in Kansas had come to the Vongsavanh house to explain.

"Your son can finish out April and May as a sophomore in the high school," the man named Anousone told Pah. "He'll need summer school to catch up, but your daughter cannot attend. She'll be nineteen next month and ineligible to return next fall. Two months is not enough time to earn a diploma. The school suggests English as a Second Language courses at the community center. Perhaps she can earn a GED someday."

Dalah's face fell flat at the news, and Meh had to excuse herself from the kitchen table. Pah thanked Anousone for explaining, but Vonlai felt sick. What was Dalah going to do? She hadn't been to school since eighth grade. She had no skills. She couldn't speak the language. Even Pah, who had a college education from France, would have to take a labor job. He had not worked as an architect for more than a decade, and America cared more about education papers than proven skill, Anousone explained. And Pah didn't have the former.

Vonlai vowed to help Dalah. This was his promise to Kavin. He'd reteach Dalah everything he learned in school and show her his books, his notes, his papers. He wasn't going to let her give up.

On his first day of school, Vonlai stood at the curb waiting for the bus. It was a cold April morning and winter had not gone away completely. His feet were cold. He didn't have anything to wear yet but his flip-flops. As he stared down at his toes and huddled inside the jacket he'd borrowed from Dakota, a clump of white landed on his foot. It disappeared in an instant. Vonlai looked up to see the snow fall, a million miniature clouds parachuting down.

He ran inside to get Dalah. "It's snowing," he shouted. "Hurry, it's snowing!"

Dalah ran outside in her sleep clothes, but it didn't matter. She cupped her hands to catch a snowflake, now fat, wet clumps that piled up quickly. She jumped to catch another and then ran to pound on the doorbell.

Pah and Meh came out, too. Vonlai stuck out his tongue to taste it, but he couldn't stand still long enough. Vannasak laughed and snapped pictures.

Pah ran to the driveway and slid to a stop at the Vongsavanhs' car. He swiped his hands down the hood to collect the thin layer of snow so he could smash the soggy mass together. "Look out," he shouted as he lobbed it at Vonlai.

"Hah," Vonlai said, dancing away from the snowball's path. "Not even close."

"You're too skinny," Dalah yelled. "It's like trying to hit a light pole!"

"Oh, yeah? I'll show you skinny!" Vonlai tackled her on the front lawn and pinned her down. The ground was mostly white now with a patchwork of green blades still holding out. Pah scooped another thin layer off the Vongsavanhs' trunk this time, and smashed it on Dalah's cheeks. Meh lay on the ground next to them and stretched out her arms to hug the falling snow.

Honk! Honk!

The school bus had pulled up. Vonlai stood up, turned, and saw a sea of stunned faces staring from the windows, their mouths dropped open like baby birds waiting for worms.

In school, the same group of boys who rode Vonlai's bus teased him every chance they got—for his flip-flops, his accent, his stick-thin body, and his *"retard snow dance on the lawn."* But there was one bright spot. The guidance counselor gave Vonlai mostly classes where a command of the language wasn't critical.

"You'll catch up over time," he'd said. *"No sense putting you in English composition just yet. Listen and learn what you can."*

So Vonlai's day was filled with physical education, art, music appreciation, current events, computer, study hall, and shop.

"What is shop?" Vonlai asked.

"Woodworking," Mr. McRae said slowly. *"Um, working with wood. Building things. With tools. From wood."*

"Yes. I understand," Vonlai said. *"It is good. Thank you very big."*

Mr. McRae smiled and showed him to class.

After a week in school, Vonlai's legs ached. He'd been sitting on the bus. Sitting in class. Sitting in Vannasak's basement to read his books, sharing everything he'd learned with Dalah. He knew the route home by now and decided to walk.

As he got close to his street, he passed a park where the neighborhood boys were playing soccer. He climbed a slide to watch, but it wasn't long until one boy recognized him.

"Hey, look, it's Ching Chong Short Dong!"

"Oh that's mature, Davidson! He's probably packing more than you, wiener boy."

"Oh, you think? Let's ask."

Vonlai jumped down and started home.

"Hey, you, Vonloo, or whatever your name is . . ." Davidson said.

Vonlai kept walking.

"Give it up, Davidson. Let's just play."

"Freaking idiot! He's too stupid to even talk." Davidson picked up the ball and hurled it at Vonlai.

It smacked him in the back of the head. Vonlai stumbled

to his knees. Davidson fell down laughing. The sting made Vonlai's eyes water, and he closed them tight. Inside his head, he was back at Na Pho, surrounded by barbed wire and the neverending stink of human sweat and waste.

Who was this American boy to take such pleasure from teasing? Had Davidson suffered greatly in his life and turned sour? Had he ever felt deep hunger—not because dinner's late, but because year after year, your body tries to survive on half the food it needs? Had he ever heard a man nearly rip away the innocence of his own flesh and blood? Had he ever said good-bye to friends whose lives were empty of opportunity?

Vonlai picked up the ball. *"Want this?"*

"Um, that'd be a yes, O wise Chinese one," Davidson said.

Vonlai dropkicked it hard. Davidson tried to catch it, but he was only able to divert its path. His face turned red as he thrust his hands in his pockets, trying to hide the sting. He chased after the ball, then stumbled and bobbled it back downfield with clumsy feet.

Vonlai kicked off his sandals and ran barefoot into the game.

He chased Davidson down in no time. Vonlai ran next to him and leaned hard against his body. He turned to cut him off, stole the ball, and flipped it easily behind his right foot. Davidson charged around Vonlai to steal it back, but Vonlai rolled it back and forth between his feet, left and right, front and back. Davidson plodded in circles to follow the ball's path. Then with a lightning flip of his foot, Vonlai kicked it between Davidson's legs and took off downfield, the other players making meager attempts to match his speed.

What a cinch to take control of the game. These American boys didn't look. They didn't really see the game. They played only to win, flailing around after the ball with no heart, not like refugees who ran to save their souls.

As Vonlai sprinted toward the goal, he imagined Khom running downfield on one side of him and Kavin running on the other. They'd pass back and forth with a light in their eyes because they knew there was nobody faster than them.

But Vonlai wasn't passing this ball to anyone.

He surged past a boy a foot taller than him and twice as thick.

Davidson's teammate guarded the goal, hopping back and forth like an angry gorilla. *"Bring it on, barefoot boy!"*

Vonlai flipped the ball behind him, turned fast, faked left, and sent it sailing toward the upper right corner. The goalie dove to block the opposite end and plunged in the dirt.

"Goooal!" the guys yelled. *"Davidson, you girl! You got whooped, big-time!"*

Vonlai said nothing as he left the field and slipped his feet back into his sandals.

He walked home as a pale half-moon pushed its way up in the sky.

That night Anousone invited the family to his place. The Lao community was waiting to meet them. Dalah piled in the Vongsavanhs' car with Virginia, Dakota, and Meh. Pah and Vonlai rode with Anousone.

On the drive over, Anousone asked about Vonlai's schooling. "You have classes you like?"

"Yes, my favorite is shop."

"Is that right? What are you making?"

"Mr. Schalker said we could choose anything for our final project." Vonlai imagined sitting under the mango tree in Na Pho, the heat and dust swirling, to tell Colonel his plan. Colonel would have smiled and nodded and never doubted.

"I'm building a skyscraper," Vonlai told Anousone. "It'll be a model for the first skyscraper in the state of Kansas!"

"Ah, big plans fill your mind," Anousone said as he pulled into his driveway. "Anybody hungry?"

"I imagine we could stand a bite," Pah said.

"Good. Tonight you eat. And tomorrow you look for work. I'll help you."

At least a hundred pairs of shoes littered the porch. Kids ran squealing through the yard and jumped over chairs. The Sirivongs added their shoes to the pile and went inside.

Aromas of foods long forgotten filled Vonlai's nose. The furniture was pushed against the walls and people sat on bamboo mats that covered the floor.

"*Sabai Di!* Hello, come in!"

In the kitchen, tin food trays covered the counters. Tender wrapped chicken and eggs steamed with mint leaves. Chopped beef with cilantro and fish sauce. Mounds of papaya salad loaded with peppers. Meh walked past each dish, taking in the colors as if she were a blind woman who'd just regained her sight. And in the center of it all, a huge bamboo basket of sticky rice.

"Have a seat," Anousone said. He led Pah and Meh to the center of a mat where a money tree sat, dollars rolled up and dangling like leaves. Anousone's daughters ducked in and out of the crowd filling drinks, serving food, and carrying away empty Styrofoam plates.

Dalah and Vonlai found a space at a corner table.

"Anything else I can get you?" Anousone asked.

"If you don't mind," Vonlai said, "I'd like to have some envelopes. And a pen, please."

"Envelopes and a pen, eh?"

"Yes, Uncle. If you can spare them."

Anousone reached into a cabinet and pulled out a box. "As you wish, Vonlai. Now I'm off to make sure your parents have plenty to eat."

Dalah popped open a can of coconut juice. She set

another in front of Vonlai. "Here, you can have this one all to yourself." Dalah pulled the sticky rice container between them and took off the lid.

The steam swirled up and warmed Vonlai's face. He scooped out a handful, rolled it into a ball, and dipped it in pepper sauce. And as they filled their bellies with sticky rice, Vonlai addressed the envelopes. He didn't stop until the box was empty and Kavin's name appeared on every one.

Afterword

My husband, Troy Anousone Manivong, spent eight months in Na Pho refugee camp in 1988, when he was eighteen years old. While Vonlai is a fictional character, many of his experiences are a reflection of stories my husband shared with me over the years. But their experiences also differ in far greater ways.

My husband's father, Nhanh Manivong, served as a lieutenant colonel in the Royal Lao Army, an ally to the United States of America. While training in Fort Leavenworth, Kansas, in 1975, as the war in Indochina was ending, Nhanh was called back to Laos, where the Communists promptly captured him and made him a prisoner of war in seminar camp #04. Anousone (my husband's given name), his mother, Dalouny, and two younger siblings joined Nhanh there, while two older siblings stayed with relatives. Anousone was in first grade at the time and never attended school again in Laos. He learned only what the Pathet Lao wanted him to learn.

After two years hidden away in the mountains of Laos in seminar camp #04, Dalouny and the younger siblings were released, but they kept Anousone so they could train him in the Communist ways. He suffered through separation from his family and untreated malaria until the Pathet Lao released him as well, three years later, in 1980, at age eleven. It was at this point that Dalouny decided to flee Laos, even though her husband remained a prisoner. She sold nearly everything she owned to hire two men to transport her and her five children across the Mekong River. Their first attempt failed because the canoe was built for only four people, and Anousone's younger brother nearly drowned, but they did make it to Thailand three days later on their second attempt.

Dalouny knew refugee camps were dangerous, especially with three daughters and no husband, so she chose instead to live illegally with relatives in Bangkok. At thirteen, Anousone worked in a factory crafting street signs so he could help alleviate the financial burden his relatives endured caring for six extra people, again never attending school. To ward off questions about his past, he told people his father was dead. For all he knew, it might be true, as there had been virtually no word of Nhanh's fate.

In 1987, after twelve years in captivity, Nhanh was

released by the Pathet Lao. He found his family in neighboring Thailand, and they all entered Na Pho refugee camp in 1988. Because of his rank in the Royal Lao Army and his alliance with America, Nhanh was confident the UNHCR would find them a new home in the United States. The Manivong family spent nearly another year in two transitional refugee camps in Bangkok and the Philippines before coming to Kansas.

My husband was nineteen when he arrived, and heartbroken to learn he was too old to attend school. Like Vonlai, it was the promise of an American education that got him through the darkest times of homelessness. After taking a labor job for two years at a pork plant in Iowa, Anousone, who now went by his American name, Troy, decided he had to learn English if he were ever to get a better job. He enrolled in ESL (English as a Second Language) classes at community centers in Kansas City. After a decade of study, Troy went on to earn his GED and an associate's degree in Information Technology. But the boom for IT jobs had waned, and Troy could not find full-time work. In 2003, he chose to go into business for himself and started his own painting and landscaping company.

Troy is now a citizen of the United States. And he hasn't shot a turkey since.

Acknowledgments

This story would not exist without Troy Anousone Manivong, whose life, and the grace with which he endured the hardships, compelled me to become a writer. An unpayable debt of gratitude is owed to him and his ever-smiling parents, Nhanh and Dalouny Manivong; to Joyce Schalker, for her cheerleading and authorly DNA, and the rest of my big, goofy, brilliant family; to Elizabeth C. Bunce, Sarah Clark, Katie Speck, and Barb Stuber for their collective insight and skill at propping me up; to Vannasak Siharath and Philicia Manivong, who shared their memories; to Kate Messner, for the title; to Michele Allen, for enduring my process; and to the skillful readers who gave the gift of their time: Jackson Duchardt, Sue Ford, Stacey Hsu, Judy Hyde, Heather Langdon, Karen Schalker, Anne and Don Sereda, Pam Stepanich, Steve Trammell, and the talented lot at Heartland Writers for

Kids and Teens. I am grateful to authors Joanna C. Scott for *Indochina's Refugees: Oral Histories from Laos, Cambodia and Vietnam*, and Bounsang Khamkeo, who opened his heart in *I Little Slave: A Prison Memoir from Communist Laos*. Deepest thanks to my agent, Ginger Knowlton; her assistant, Tracy Marchini; and my editor, Rosemary Brosnan, for making this all real.